WILLOW ROSE

First edition
ISBN (paperback): 979-8-9927805-5-0
ISBN (hardcover): 979-8-9927805-4-3
ISBN (digital): 979-8-9927805-7-4

Developmental Editing by Laura Williams
Copyediting by Ciera Cox
Copyediting by Lily Edgerton
Proofreading by Melanie Scott
Cover art and interior design by Nuno Moreira, NMDESIGN

WILLOW ROSE

M. KEVIN HAYDEN

MUSE
of the MOON
BOOKS

MORE STORY ... MORE MUSIC.

Amazon Music

Apple Music

Spotify

YouTube

For the loved ones at or already beyond their new *beginning*…

we miss you.

"What is in a name? That which we call a rose, by any other name, would smell just as sweet."

— William Shakespeare

CHAPTER ONE

Dr. Alder Peony is working his third twenty-four-hour shift this week. He signed the contract. There's no use complaining.

Like many remote Critical Access Hospitals, Morningstar Falls Medical Center pays big bucks to lure doctors to places that would otherwise have no access to care. Alder's plan was simple: take the money, chip away at student loans (and a few other debts), and cruise through what he assumed would be an easy gig.

Then there's reality.

MFMC's ER isn't as hectic as a city hospital, but when you're the only doc on shift, the grind wears you down. Patients trickle in over the twenty-four hours—never enough at once to call it busy, but just steady enough to keep rest out of reach. A dripping faucet. Always one more patient.

He didn't sleep or eat much in Chicago or Las Vegas either, but at least here, there's time to piss.

The exhaustion comes and goes. Some days are worse than others. But the real wrench? The loneliness.

Harsh fluorescent lights clash with the subdued green walls and tan curtains of the exam rooms. The headache-inducing brightness pushes Alder to his feet, and he switches off half of them, leaving the room in a muted calm.

"Better," he whispers to himself.

The theme song to *Sanford and Son* plays softly from a television in one of the examination rooms.

It's four a.m., and Alder sits at the central station, scribbling on a chart. The only nurse, Faith, walks toward him, leading his only patient—thank God—over to say something.

The sweet ninety-year-old Mrs. Dodd shimmies, holding onto Faith's crooked elbow and bearing a wide grin. She talks before getting to him. The image of her toddling to the *Sanford and Son* theme nearly sends him into exhausted hysterics.

"Dr.—Dr. P!"

Mrs. Dodd releases Faith's arm, then reaches out for Alder. He stands and accepts her hand.

"Yes, Mrs. Dodd? Are you feeling better?"

"Why, yes, I am, thanks to you! I can't believe how constipated I was." She waves her hand. "It just hung there … I thought I would just die! I figured, if only I could reach right up there, I could get things moving."

She tilts her head and pats the back of Alder's hand. "I didn't have that magic touch … You are such a sweetheart."

Alder's sleep-deprived brain lags. At first it fails to process that Mrs. Dodd is gripping his bare hand, likely with the same hand she'd used in her attempt to dislodge her own impacted poop—a task which ultimately fell to him.

He watches her decrepit little fingers squeeze his forearm, barely able to support herself.

Alder's glance swings up from his hands to find Mrs. Dodd beaming at him, her face a mixture of joy and relief. She'll sleep tonight.

Oh, what the hell, he thinks. My life's already up shit creek.

"It was my pleasure, Mrs. Dodd!" Alder says.

The words echo in his head, and he cringes. What kind of shit is that to say—*my pleasure*? After fishing out impacted poo? Now everyone here thinks I'm some kind of weirdo. I need to sleep.

He exhales and leans against the counter. Thankfully, tonight's shaping up to be not too crazy.

In the Emergency Department, the words *slow* or *quiet* are taboo, jinxes uttered only by accidental slips of the tongue. Saying either is like sounding the Horns of the Apocalypse. So instead, one would say it's not crazy—or say nothing at all.

Mrs. Dodd shuffles away, with Faith's help. "He is handsome—are you two married?"

Faith's face flushes. "No, Mrs. Dodd, we're not." She tucks a strand of hair behind her ear and leans in with a smirk. "But I agree. Very handsome."

"Tall, dark, and handsome," Mrs. Dodd says. She pauses, then whispers with a sly grin, "Did I mention dark? And handsome?"

Faith chortles, covering her mouth. "Yes, yes, you did, Mrs. Dodd!"

No, at thirty-nine, Alder is not married. At twenty-six, he came close to carrying Jessie Langhart across the threshold. She was beautiful, smart—his med school classmate. Steel-blue eyes, curly brunette hair cascading to just above her delicate shoulders. Her eyes matched the sky on a clear day. Hypnotic. Like everything else in his past, he messed that up.

Twelve years gone. It's late November 2005. His last two five-year plans fell apart. Now, he's closing in on a third round.

A Black man in the middle of nowhere, which is better than being a Black man in some places.

* * *

The ER is small, with five beds and three entrances:

• Triage, on the north side, opens into the main ER lobby, which connects to the hospital.

• The ambulance bay, to the east, is where EMTs roll in their patients.

• A secondary hospital entrance, on the west side, links the ER to the rest of the facility via a conjoined hallway.

Most of the doors stay locked, controlled by automatic sensors. Outside of triage, the main hallway stretches toward the rest of the hospital, a lonely corridor leading deeper into the silence—and to the

ER-side entrance.

In Room One, Roland, the night emergency-room tech, flips the TV from *Sanford and Son* to the cable news station. The clipped tones of a seasoned anchor fill the room.

At the nurses' station, Alder scrubs his hands up to the elbows, listening to the anchor's voice.

"It appeared out of nowhere, baffling astronomers worldwide. Comet C/2005 L3—also known as Comet Goodwin—named after the backyard astronomer who first spotted it."

The anchor chuckles. "Well … not exactly an astronomer."

Alder glances over his shoulder at the TV. His interest flickers. Something about this thing unsettles him deep down. Years ago, he'd prayed for a sign—one that would warn him when his number was up. Time to pay the fiddler.

He can't shake the feeling that the sign is now painted across the sky. The wide tail spans about thirty percent of it, day or night.

The screen shifts to an interview with Luna Goodwin. Her boisterous Australian accent cuts through the hum of the room.

"I was just in me yard, right? Looked up and thought, crikey—that wasn't theh before. I was bloody knackered, reckoned maybe I was seein' things. But nope, clear as day—movin' north. Cleared across the sky in minutes, yeh? Neveh seen anythin' like it."

She giggles, looking skyward.

"Snapped an upward pic of me dog with me digi-cam, and wouldn't ya know it? First image of the bloody thing."

Onscreen, Luna inverts a can of beer—drinking the last bit—then lifts it in a casual toast toward the sky.

The anchor returns, his voice professional but laced with intrigue.

"Experts at NASA have confirmed that the comet, discovered only two days ago, is an anomaly. Astronomers usually detect comets long before they're visible. This one appeared suddenly—unlike anything previously recorded and defying all previous assumptions about our universe. Its extraordinary proximity to Earth and spectacularly long tail have made it visible at all hours in both hemispheres—an unprecedented event in modern astronomy."

He pauses, leaning into the mystery.

"NASA has raised concerns about the comet's proximity. Fragments from its tail—meteors and meteorites—may survive entry into our atmosphere. Most should burn up harmlessly, but there are reports of meteorites reaching the surface. Analysis is ongoing to determine the composition of the meteorites, which may originate from outside of our own solar system. There's also concern about the comet's tail interfering with electronics and communications. This disruption may continue to affect supply chains and could even hinder access to emergency services. Scientists believe changes in the Earth's upper atmosphere play a role, but the exact causes remain unclear."

The camera shifts to the male coanchor, who attempts levity.

"Well, looks like I'll finally get some use out of that telescope collectin'"—the screen stutters, audio distorts—"d-d-d-duuuuuust in my closet. Or wait, do I even need one?"

His colleague smirks. "No, Jim, I don't reckon you do."

A beat passes. The anchor shuffles papers and clears his throat.

Jim continues, "Wow—so lucky. She just snapped the first photo and now a celebrity?" He shakes his head. "Good for her!"

A brief, awkward pause.

"That wraps up your early news. Stay safe, and good morning. Stay tuned for *Get Up, Columbia.*"

*　　*　　*

Alder finishes the chart. He wants to get at least an hour of shuteye. He's not driving far this morning, but he can barely walk five feet, let alone drive five miles. He shouldn't even be caring for patients.

With his dominant left hand idly spinning a pen, Alder gazes blankly into space, dreaming of his warm bed.

Faith's honeyed voice floats over his shoulder just as he drops Mrs. Dodd's chart in the bin.

"Dr. P. A new patient. His hand got caught in an auger. It's a mess."

Faith's voice always softens the blow of bad news—usually with a side of pumpkin cream-cheese muffins.

When her words brush his ear, something inside him settles. He can't say no to her.

And, yes, he finds her beautiful too. In another life, Alder would've asked her out on first contact. There's something in her presence—serene, steady—that calms his storm. When he meets her kind eyes, the past doesn't weigh quite so much.

Gentle curves accentuate Faith's five-feet-eight-inch frame, and a single dimple punctuates her olive-toned cheek when she smiles. Her soft brown eyes are slightly upturned, framed by lashes that catch the light when she laughs. Her scrubs almost always lean toward gentle purples—subtle, wistful shades that seem to bloom on her. She's a perfect, purple presence in Alder's dreams.

He gets clumsy, awkward, when lost in those eyes—especially when they're paired with that smile. It's why he keeps jokes to a minimum while doing procedures. He'd look like a clown fumbling with forceps, trying to hold it together.

Yeah, that giggling smile is dangerous when sharp objects are involved. A simple three-centimeter laceration could turn into a gaping axe wound. *My bad, sir!*

But more than anything, it's Faith's voice that gets him. Not overly sultry, not too sweet—serenity in a sound. A voice you feel before you hear it—the perfect accompaniment to her eyes and uni-dimpled smile.

Maybe in another lifetime. In this one, Alder doesn't feel anyone deserves the pain of getting too close to him.

A gruff male voice erupts from the triage area.

"Aaaaagh! I was digging a well! Aaaaaaagh! Please, knock me out! Can't you just knock me out? DAMMIIIIIT! Tssssshh!"

Faith jogs to the triage area, her soft, gentle voice cutting through the ruckus as she attempts to calm the man and get more information.

"We're going to take good care of you! Tell me what happened?"

"Aaaaagh. I just said ... the auger went haywire ... Fuuuu—!"

Alder P. is not getting that hour of sleep. *Figures.*

*   *   *

Dr. Jennings rolls in right on time at five a.m. Suspenders, silver mustache, silver wire-framed spectacles. He has coffee in hand and is unbothered, as usual. Even in chaos, he moves like a man with nowhere urgent to be.

Alder gives him the rundown, which consists of nothing because it was *not crazy*, until the end.

The last patient is in a ground ambulance, tearing toward Duluth General, *Dukes of Hazzard* style. Alder tied off his gushing wrist artery, so he'll live to meet the hand surgeon tasked with untangling the shredded mess of tendons and bone. A helicopter would have been ideal, but the damned comet grounded most air travel worldwide. Why would a man be drilling a well at three a.m.? That's someone else's question to ask. Alder's just glad to hand over the keys.

Since Comet Goodwin's arrival, a sheen of strangeness has blanketed the world—people included.

Jennings nods, looks over the rim of his glasses, and smirks. "Night, kid."

Night shifters always say goodnight after a shift, no matter that it's just before sunrise.

Alder reaches under the station desk for his backpack, slinging it over a shoulder. He pauses in thought—then discreetly glances back at Faith.

She's also gathering her things, tucking stray supplies into her canvas craft-store tote, the one she always carries, patched and well-worn. When she looks up, their eyes meet. Not a collision, not a sparking explosion. Their eyes connect with the softness of a feather settling onto grass.

Her lip curls slightly. She tries to rein it in, but her cheek dimple betrays her. All the while, her eyes linger on Alder's, inviting.

Alder is not one to project his wants onto someone else, but his heart still revs up at the thought. He tries to control his uneven breaths.

Don't appear thirsty, Aldi.

Alder searches for an escape from the impending awkwardness. He diverts his gaze to the tray of her baked goodies. He plucks the last pumpkin muffin—his favorite.

"Breakfast and dinner," he says with a half smirk.

Faith's cheeks turn pink, and she covers her lips with her fingertips. She always blushes when people appreciate her baking, going from alluring to adorable in a beat. And there goes his heart … thumping wildly.

"Goodnight, Dr. P," she says.

Her voice! So soft, it lingers in the air, buzzing in his mind like sparkling white noise.

She's not done. "Get home safe, OK?"

Alder clears his throat. "—Night, Faith." He shakes his head; his cool palm feels good pressed against his flushed forehead.

Faith hovers just a second longer. Alder feels it—a pause heavy with unspoken words.

Well? Say something, man!

Faith only smiles, wiping her hands on her hips as she turns for the door. "Night."

Alder watches her leave and attempts to break his stalling pattern with her, then realizes that he will be leaving soon.

Faith isn't a toss-away. And he doesn't want that anymore, anyway. Those years are behind him. He's been clean—and on the lame road—

for two years now. The self-loathing? It's manageable there.

Still, inviting someone into his mess is unimaginable. His yuck, though now more controlled, is still a yuck nonetheless. He wouldn't knowingly do that to another person.

That's why he keeps a distance, even if it's a narrow one. And he'll settle into it, like he always does. Sometimes he wonders what it would be like to just … let someone in.

*   *   *

Outside, the cold grabs Alder by the ribs. Rushing out the door yesterday, he forgot his coat and only wore his green hooded sweatshirt. His thin, washed-out green scrubs, pilfered from the OR on his last contract, are underneath.

He curses under his breath as he slides into the cloth driver's seat of his burgundy '96 Honda Civic hatchback. The tan automatic shoulder belt groans its way across his chest, pressing his cold scrubs against his skin. It was mild when he started the shift twenty-four hours ago, but in true Minnesota fashion, the weather had a change of heart.

Forecasters predict a major snowstorm to hit in the next two days, right before his next twenty-four-hour shift. It emerged unexpectedly, much like Comet Goodwin.

The Civic hesitates. Then, finally, the engine sputters to life.

Alder points skyward, thanking the heavens beyond the broad tail of Comet Goodwin.

This car carried him through residency and another five years. It's seen better days, but debt ensures he'll be holding onto it for the foreseeable future.

He's tired and needs a couple of days away from this tiny hospital, carved into the piney wilderness off Gunmetal Road.

The boreal forests are deep and endless. Pines stretch toward the sky, silent and watchful. Most of the land in this area belongs to the proud Ojibwe people—as it always has.

Alder shivers in the forty-two-degree chill. He just needs to make it home—cabin, bed, unconscious before the sun—before that creepy comet clears the horizon in the east.

He clicks on the car stereo. A deep, pleasant male voice fills the cabin.

"Gooooood morning, folks. This is Bart Ellis, and you are listening to Behold a Dark Horse!"

Bart lets the silence stretch, then stutters, his voice sharpening with frustration.

"I-I don't know how many of you agree or disagree—and I'm gonna get to your calls shortly—but-but this is bull-plop. Do-do … do they really think we're idiots? That we won't demand answers? A-a good friend, huh? Comets, a good friend, don't just appear at your door uninvit—" Bart's voice cuts out.

Then, a jarring noise, like a massive zipper ripping open.

Ziiiip.

Then—nothing. No white noise. No static. Just silence. A dead, heavy silence.

"Fuckin' comet," Alder says under his breath. "Tsssh."

Alder can only brave five seconds of this eerie silence before the hairs on his arms stand up. The mania root that is this comet twists beneath his world, ready to sprout and shatter the ground beneath his feet.

He presses the CD button on his car stereo and slides in a disc. He skips forward to "Ill Wind," the Lee Morgan version. Probably a bad idea, considering he can barely keep his eyes from sliding shut, but right now, he needs calm. This song is the equivalent of melodic balm, soothing the edges of his fatigue.

As the car warms, he wipes the fogging windshield and looks upward. There it is: Comet Goodwin's tail, a jagged pall of green fire stretching from northeast to southwest across the predawn sky.

The comet itself remains just below the horizon, hidden from view, but its presence is undeniable. Soon, it will rise with the sun—its eerie companion in the morning light.

From the heavy meteor showers, the tail flickers. At moments, it feels like being encased in a glass dome, watching blazing drops of liquid fire roll and tumble, their light reflecting on the curved surface.

No one saw this thing coming. Two days ago, it wasn't there. Now, the closest comet in recorded history looms overhead.

Alder exhales, unease curling in his gut. It feels like an omen. A judgment. He doesn't know why—it just does.

Maybe it's the way the green tail smears across the sky like a ghostly, shimmering brushstroke. Too vivid. Too alive.

The darkness runs deep in boreal Minnesota, even in the moments before dawn. Goodwin's tail creates a strange light in the sky, but the shadows remain strong here.

Alder's warm headlights carve a thin path west along Gunmetal Road. In the distance, the darkness absorbs the beam. Tall pines flank the narrow two-lane road, their silhouettes forming a cathedral-like shape that obscures the purple-green sky ahead.

Alder struggles to keep his eyes open.

A flicker—Alder's foot snags while stepping up a sidewalk curb. He feels a sudden weightlessness as his head dips.

He's asleep. Dreaming.

"Shit!"

His body lurches. Eyes snap open.

Both feet slam down. One—thankfully—hits the brake.

Squeeeeeeeer.

The car shrieks—tires skidding—coming to rest three feet from a massive bull elk. The faint smell of cooked brake pads seeps into the vehicle.

The elk doesn't flinch. It doesn't even twitch. Its dark eyes lock onto the sky, antlers angled back, as if bolted into an invisible, tilted yoke. The only movement is the expansion and contraction of its ribs. Its breath billows from its hanging mouth like a locomotive. A thick strand of saliva trembles like a plucked guitar string, then snaps on its way to the dull gray road.

These elks are rarely, if ever, seen in this area.

"Shit ... Shit. SHIT!" Alder white-knuckles the steering wheel.

His heart thumps violently against the walls of his chest, heaving like it needs more room.

He sits frozen, his amped-up, exhausted brain trying to process what just happened, what to do next.

The sight of this creature slams into him, causing a full-body recoil. Pure dread, the kind that stops you dead in your tracks. The kind where you can't run, you can't breathe. A sudden itch in the center of your back.

As his brain reboots, his first logical thought arrives—lean on the horn.

Meeeep.

He doesn't lean long. The sound echoes off Lake Waaseyaa to his left, then bounces back from the endless forest of pines and conifers to his right. The sound ripples through the stillness, amplifying his panic.

It's like standing in the center of a gladiator pit, waiting for a gargantuan opponent while mouth-breathing onlookers gasp. In this case, there is no crowd. Just the hush of trees. And yet, he feels watched—by the breadth of the wilderness itself.

Alder takes control of his breathing, trying to calm himself.

The elk still doesn't react.

Then, its eyes widen.

Its head tilts back a foot more.

And then—

A blinding white flash.

The world ignites, searing a frozen blue silhouette of the elk into Alder's retinas.

"The fu—!"

Before he can finish, a thunderous crack detonates the morning air. Pressure punches and rumbles in his chest and skull. His car rocks, the ground trembles.

Then comes the elk's bugle.

A raw, deafening sound—laced within, but louder than the explosion itself.

It rips through Alder's skull, reverberating into the night.

"SHIT! Rasshole! Fuck, fuck!"

He can't even hear his last *fuck*, swallowed by the noise. His lips move, but the sound is buried.

Alder reflexively flops over into the passenger seat, arms shielding his head as his ears ring. His legs remain tangled under the steering wheel, locking him into an awkward half-twist.

The sound continues until the driver's window shatters inward, sending a spray of tiny glass shards toward his body. The fragments rain down like jagged dice, skittering with clicks across the carpeted floor mats.

Alder is frozen, unable to will his body to move an inch.

A sharp, overpowering smell floods his senses—alien, unplaceable, and disturbingly vivid. It's like rust, pepper, and oranges. This and the ringing in his ears create a bizarre combination that only deepens his disorientation, unraveling his tenuous grip on reality.

For a moment, he questions whether he's still in his body or if his soul has slipped into another plane of existence.

His eyes dart frantically in the darkness, searching for something to anchor him, something familiar. A faint glow catches his attention, a dim light from somewhere—just enough to illuminate the Honda logo on the glove compartment. It's the only thing that makes sense.

Alder sits up, his movements tentative, but he feels ... nothing. No pain, no soreness. He scans his body with quick, trembling hands and finds no immediate sign of trauma.

He peers at his reflection in the rearview mirror. Hard to make out, but his face is still his own. His breath fogs the glass. Then his gaze shifts beyond it.

The sky looks wrong, as it has for the last two days. A strange, dark grey-green, shimmering with an unnatural, billowy scribble that drifts across the predawn heavens.

A faint glow emanates from under the car, pooling around it like an otherworldly mist. The sight sharpens his awareness, and his gaze shifts to the windshield—completely cobwebbed with cracks—opaque and useless. The driver's window is nothing but an empty frame, jagged glass edges gleaming faintly in the strange light.

He instinctively reaches to his side for his Motorola Razr flip phone. Opening it, he presses the power button. Nothing. Dead. Just like the world around him.

His car's engine and battery are both unresponsive.

The only light source is that faint surrounding glow.

After a minute, his shiver returns, more violent this time—fueled by both his terror and the biting cold. He clumsily holds down the volume and power buttons on his cell phone.

It doesn't reset. A black paperweight.

"Rasshole," he mutters under his breath.

He takes a few deep breaths, steeling himself before stepping out— slowly, tentatively.

He steadies his breathing. His head swivels, scanning for danger. Cautiously, he leans forward, peering around the front of the vehicle. Other than the glass, the car is undamaged. Golden flecks shimmer on the bumper and ground, glowing like embers.

The elk lies lifeless in the center of the road. A quarter-sized hole marks its side, neat and clean—no blood. Just … a hole.

The soft glow surrounding the car dims just before everything plunges into darkness. The headlights flicker back on, and "Ill Wind" resumes, drifting through the broken window.

Alder's phone buzzes to life in his hand.

"Hello, Moto."

With numb, cold hands, Alder levers it open.

It reads 5:40 a.m. Battery: 10%

No signal. Just the time and the fact that his phone will die soon. Not that it would be of much use with more battery. The signal out here is spotty as is.

He flips the phone closed to preserve the remaining battery and finds that the elk is gone. Vanished. No blood. No gold flecks. No light. Everything, gone—only the shattered windows remain as proof that shit went down.

Alder brushes glass from the front seat and slides back in. He turns the key.

Tshh-tssh-tssh.

No luck. The engine won't turn over. Alder blows into his hands.

The road is empty. His teeth chatter violently. As his adrenaline tide wanes, his limbs become heavy, and his mind clouds from exhaustion.

"This can't be real ... this can't be real ... this can't be real." His voice shakes, matching his hands.

Dawn creeps in. Alder sits and waits for a passerby that never comes.

He fumbles with his phone: X signal. 6:45 a.m.

It feels like he's been out here for eight hours, but it's been just over one.

His shiver calms—a dangerous sign. His body temperature is dropping, and if he stays like this much longer, severe hypothermia will take hold. He's already exhausted, and the cold is leeching what little heat he has left. He can barely form clear thoughts.

"Please, please ... I'll do whatever you want up there ... please."

Alder clasps his hands. He only feels pressure, the numbing cold dulling his sense of touch. He isn't a religious man, but his mother's devotion lingers in his subconscious, keeping him from true atheism. He has to believe in Something. *Something* has kept him alive until now, and he hopes that Something will keep it up.

One more try, then I walk. Out there.

That's the deal he makes with himself. He will turn the engine over in one more, likely futile, attempt.

Tssst-tsst-tsst.

The engine sputters to life.

Close to tears, Alder thanks *Something* in a thick voice.

His windshield is a shattered mess—barely any visibility.

Then he sees it, a palm-sized, unbroken piece of glass in the lower left. It will have to do.

His cabin is two miles away. Just get there. A hot shower, then sleep.

Alder's shiver worsens, draining what little heat he has left and intensifying his exhaustion.

Shower. Bed. Maybe food. The main priority being the shower.

He has three days off. The glass can be dealt with another day.

Alder slaps his own face, sharp enough to sting. But with his hand gone numb in the cold, it feels like someone else hit him.

As for the elk, and whatever the hell that explosion was—

"Aldi. Wake up! Snap out of this!"

He tries to convince himself. "Hallucination … a dream."

Alder knows he fell asleep behind the wheel. He sleep-tripped during a hypnogogic dream, and this was a hypnogogic hallucination. The elk, all of this shit—illusions created by his fatigued mind.

He shakes his head. The simplest explanation: sleep deprivation. Hallucinations.

"Meteorite." He locks onto the theory.

A meteorite, a weird-ass hallucination, and sleep deprivation, nothing more. That's what he needs to believe. That's what gets him home.

He grips the wheel, breathes deep, and inches forward, hunched over and peering through the palm-sized viewhole.

Alder mutters to himself, "Makes sense ... Get to bed, Aldi—before you lose your shit!"

*   *   *

As Alder veers onto the path toward his long-term rental cabin, dawn overtakes the night. With the sunrise, Comet Goodwin's coma appears from the northeast. This is the body of the comet which shines a blazing bright white. He has been trying not to look at it directly, pretend it's not there. The very sight of it gnaws at the core of his being.

The brisk air assaults his left side through the broken window. He shifts the car into park and opens the door simultaneously. He stumbles frantically to the sanctuary of indoors.

Upon opening the door, Alder is greeted by a comforting warmth in the one-room cabin, equipped with central heating. He makes his way to the bathroom to start his shower, closing the door behind him before heading to the kitchen. Alder fills a large glass with water from the tap and drinks it down in one go, as if he'd been wandering in the desert.

He claws off his muted green hooded sweatshirt and scrubs, tossing them to the floor.

The shiver returns, but is overshadowed by the thought of relief— that shower.

Thick, white steam billows from the bathroom, accompanied by the faint sound of running water. Warm humidity curls around him like a blissful embrace. He steps into the shower, and it takes two full minutes before his teeth stop chattering and his shiver finally melts away.

His breath evens. His pulse steadies. Calm takes hold.

Water sprays through Alder's tightly coiled hair, massaging his scalp before trickling down his brown neck and chest. This feels like heaven— almost. The best shower he's ever had, interrupted only by stinging, paranoid eye-openings.

The occasional pinecone thud from outside—he's nearly used to it by now. But after the madness of this morning, the sound pops off the windows differently. Everything is badness until proven otherwise.

Even the silence feels heavy, but not enough to smother the sense of a dark presence.

His respite from the cold had made him file the strange morning in the back of his mind. But as his body stabilizes and the threat of hypothermia fades, his brain shifts priorities—back to anxiety. It needs something to do, especially at bedtime.

Alder steps onto the rugged bathmat. His goosebumps have retreated. The towel feels strange against his pruney fingertips. He dries off and pulls on an old pair of jogging pants and a faded Chicago Cubs tee-shirt.

That cream-cheese pumpkin muffin will have to hold him. It's bedtime.

His head throbs as he walks over to the kitchen and palms a bottle of Tylenol. He rattles it next to his ear, then hesitates—wishing they were Oxys. He sets them on the counter next to a sobriety chip—two years. He picks it up and inspects it.

Alder closes his eyes, rolling the chip between his fingers. Muscle memory.

He lets out a breath, blowing off the craving. *These will do.*

Why would anyone invite back the thing they're escaping when they've been winning?

It makes little sense—a part of the disease—but he's been winning for two plus years now. He tosses two of the over-the-counter tabs onto his tongue, washing them down with the strange-tasting tap water from the cabin.

Alder grimaces. "Ugh."

At 8:30 a.m., Alder draws his room-darkening shades and tumbles into bed. As he pulls the comforter over his body, his legs shuffle under the sheets, an unconscious motion of bliss. This doesn't last long, as his eyes fall shut mid-kick.

A few moments later, he jerks awake—his heart pounding for an instant—but the pull of exhaustion is too strong. His eyes close again, and he's off into deep sleep.

*   *   *

Pitch darkness.

"Hmph?" Alder jolts awake, disoriented by the oppressive blackness. His arms flail, brushing against his pillow, before he realizes he's in bed.

Leaning over, he fumbles for the lamp switch. It squeaks, then clicks, casting a dim, sore light that makes his pupils constrict. He squints and looks around the one-room cabin. Outside, the wind howls and pinecones slap against the window.

Alder rolls out of bed. His ankles are stiff as he shuffles to the kitchen. Grabbing a carton of orange juice, he downs a pint straight from the container. He coughs at the end, the pulp scratching his throat.

He glances at the clock on the wall. Three a.m. He lingers in the kitchen, unsure of what to do next. His mind feels foggy, stuck between sleep and wakefulness and unable to grasp what, if anything, needs to be done.

As he approaches the side window of the cabin, he yawns and mutters, "Crazy drea—" His words are cut off as he pulls the shade and sees the damaged windshield and shattered window.

"Meteori—yeah!" Alder releases the edge of the shade and walks back to the fridge. A barely audible knock makes him freeze in the center of the cabin. When it stops, he thinks—hopes—it's just a raccoon or something.

Tap-tap-tap.

Pause.

Tap ... tap.

Alder gasps.

That wasn't the wind. Nor an animal.

Alder responds, timid at first, "Yeah?"

No one answers.

Tap-tap-tap-tap-tap. Pause.

Alder calls out again, lowering his register. "Who's there?" He clears his throat. "Hello?"

Tap-tap-tap.

He creeps toward the door, pulls the chain over, and leans in, peeking through the peephole.

Nothing.

Only darkness, faint moonlight, and the ethereal green glow of the comet's tail filtering through the trees.

Then—

Tap-tap-tap.

Sharper this time. Small knuckles. Right against the lower part of the door.

Alder frowns, looking through the peephole again. Still nothing.

He exhales, then creaks the door open, keeping the chain on.

At first, he sees no one—until his gaze drops.

A tiny blonde head.

It's a little girl, no older than seven. She looks up at him, green eyes wide, smiling. She waves as if she knows him.

It feels like someone has spilled ice water down Alder's spine, kicking his functions into flight mode.

It's three a.m.

A paralysis, now all too familiar after the last twenty-four hours, stills Alder.

The little girl pushes at the door, her small hands pressing against the wood as she grins. The chain rattles, the only thing keeping her out.

"Wait … Wait! Where are your parents?" Alder asks, his voice low and cautious. "Hello? Who are you?"

The little girl points at him, her finger unwavering, but doesn't say a word.

"Hey ... who are you? What's your name?" he tries again, his voice tightening with unease. "Yo!"

She points at him once more, then shrugs with an exaggerated motion. "Willow!" she says, her voice almost singsong.

"OK ... Willow ... you can't come in here. Where are your parents?" Alder looks around, sweeping as much area as he can through a cracked, still-chained door. All that he sees is the moonlight pouring through the pines, the ground carpeted by glowing fog.

He takes a four-second deep breath, closes the door—and, against his intuition, slides off the chain. Alder pauses.

Black man. Middle of nowhere. A little white girl at three a.m.! Where the hell are her parents?

He grunts. *Made-for-TV-ass bullshit. Ugh!*

Every instinct says to keep the door shut. Walk away. Let this be someone else's problem.

Alder exhales. He groans as he grips the knob and opens the door, continuing his survey as it creaks open. His eyes pan up, down, and around, before landing on the pint-sized Willow. She stands there, disturbingly unaffected by the fact that she is alone in the woods.

That last eerie realization tightens Alder's grip on the knob. Every instinct tells him to shut the door, call the sheriff, and go back to bed.

Then he looks down at her again—green eyes bright like emeralds, even in the darkness. She grins widely, her own light source, it seems.

"WILLOW!"

A panicked female voice calls out, drawing nearer. "WILLOW!"

A woman who looks to be in her forties emerges from the woods, her silhouette stark against the eerie glow of the night. Above her, the waxing crescent moon gleams through the translucent veil of Comet Goodwin's tail, its greenish light diffused like sheer curtains draped across the sky. The comet streaks brighter than the Milky Way, its luminous trail crossing the galaxy's band, forming a jagged, uneven X in the heavens.

The woman's frantic gaze locks onto the cabin door where Willow stands. She starts toward it, her steps quickening with urgency.

Relief and unease are at war within Alder as he watches her. He glances to the right of the door, where his protective nightstick rests—pragmatic caution in boreal Minnesota. After all, he's a Black man in the middle of the woods.

Right upside the head. That's the strategy he has planned, should he ever need it.

"And you are?" Alder's voice deepens as he puffs his chest.

"Clara!" the woman replies, breathless from running. She reaches for Willow, pulling her close. "This is my daughter! She must've gotten lost."

"Lost? At this hour? Lady, it's three o'clock in the morning!"

Clara raises a hand, her voice apologetic. "Please … I'm sorry. She gets out sometimes—an explorer. Always claiming she's trying to find herself. She's a seven-year-old that sounds eighteen—am I right?" She tilts her head. "I am so sorry!"

Alder's fingers twitch on the doorknob. Something isn't adding up.

He exhales hard through his nose. "Maybe I ought to call the sheriff."

"No!" Clara's hand shoots up again, urgency in her tone. "No—please, there's no need for that. Tell him, Willow. Tell him I'm your mama."

Willow looks up at her. "Yeah, she's my … mama," Willow says, her tone tinged with slight confusion.

Alder's suspicion lingers, but exhaustion presses heavier. The bed is calling, and he's too drained to deal with this any longer.

"I understand. Please, be careful. Goodnight," he says with a wave.

"Goodnight, Mr. …"

"Alder." He snickers. "Alder Peony."

"Mister Peony," Clara echoes, offering a smirk.

"Doc—never mind. Alder's fine."

"Goodnight, Mr. Peony, and again—I'm so sorry for all of this!"

"Alder is OK. Never mind, it's all good," he replies, watching Clara and Willow disappear into the fog between the trees.

As he closes the door, his eyes linger on their silhouettes until they vanish into the woods.

Where they're staying is unclear. There isn't another cabin for at least a mile, as far as he knows. He's never seen Clara or Willow before, and they've never been to the hospital.

Alder rarely forgets a face, even in passing. Yet despite that, there's something familiar about Willow. Not visually—something deeper. A presence can be as familiar as a face or a voice.

Back to bed for a few hours, deal with the car in the morning. Whenever the time comes, he'll make his way to Hell for being so passive about that little girl, if she was in danger.

Alder's DOMA—*Day Off My Ass*—was officially over. At least today, his second and *actual* day off, would give him time to get his car glass fixed.

As he lies in bed, Alder thinks to himself, *I really am a shitheel. No question. Should've called the sheriff. A place for me is being prepared in the depths, for sure. Mama is up there, throwin' her shoe from heaven.*

He reaches for the landline, yawning.

"Straight to Hell you go Aldi," he mutters.

He's out before his fingers even touch the receiver—drifting into sleep, wrapped in self-loathing.

CHAPTER TWO

"How much?" Alder asks, brow furrowed.

"Nine hundred bucks ... didn't stutter," says Aubrey—at least, that's what his patch reads. He is puffed up with self-importance.

The sign out front reads *Konrad's*.

Alder stares. Nine hundred? For some glass? The number hits like a slap. His eyes flick to a junked Honda Civic with slightly tinted windows in the lot. It's clear where his nine hundred bucks are going. A switcheroo.

"Seriously?"

"Take it or leave it, chief."

Alder winces. Aubrey's smugness burns.

Didn't stutter, huh?

So much for small-town charm. Then again, what small town? This felt more like a vortex—reservation land and scattered outposts swirling and clinging together like driftwood—rather than anything resembling a community.

"Fine. Whatever. How long?"

"A week." Aubrey flashes a sardonic grin, revealing a snaggled front tooth.

"A week? I need it tomorrow," Alder shoots back, heat rising in his voice.

Aubrey shrugs, that grin making it sting all the more. "For twelve hundred, I'll have it done by the end of the day."

Alder feels the heat rush to his face, despite the chill outside. He wipes at his beard, trying to keep calm.

"So you can? You just ... woooow. Fine."

Reaching into his pocket, he pulls out six hundred dollars—everything he has on him. "Will you take a check for the rest?"

Aubrey shakes his head without hesitation. "Cash only. But I'll take that six for now, and we can settle up when you pick it up."

Grinding his teeth, Alder hands over the money. Aubrey snatches it, immediately starting his count with a snicker.

"We'll get you visible, chief. Pleasure." He turns and walks off, leaving Alder standing there.

"Dare I even ask ... you got a loaner?" Alder calls after him.

Aubrey pinky-points at a beat-up Buick Skyhawk parked near the garage. The car looks like it hasn't moved in years.

He twirls the finger in the air. "Keys're in it."

Feeling defeated, Alder saunters over to the rusting heap and sighs. He just needs to get to the bank and back.

The rusty door whines as he opens it. It smells musty and damp—even on this cold, arid November morning. *Is my tetanus up to date?*

Sliding the key into the ignition, he twists.

Squiiiiiirrrrrrrrr.

The engine protests, wheezing like it hasn't started in years. He tries again.

Squiiiiiirrrr—bumpbumpbump.

Alder whispers, "Rasshole."

Squiiirr—bumpbumpbump—grumblegrumblegrumble.

On the third try, the engine coughs to life, but shudders as if it might give out at any second. A blast of frigid air hits Alder's face from the vents. He groans, sliding the heat switch all the way to the right. The cold air keeps coming.

He lets the old beater run for a minute, watching his breath fog the air, then shifts into reverse. The car lurches as he backs out of the lot and heads down the road.

*   *   *

A long, restless day.

The car windows are fixed. Sort of. As Alder drives back to the cabin, he recognizes the slight tint on the glass—it's from that junker in the lot. Figures. Backwoods robbery, plain and simple.

It's just past seven p.m. Darkness is settling. A waxing gibbous moon hangs low, with Comet Goodwin's tail casting an eerie, twinkling green twilight over the treetops.

As Alder drives down the long road toward his cabin, a tug of unease grips him. The image of the woman and little girl wandering through the woods still lingers in his mind. They didn't seem threatening, but something felt off.

And then there's the meteorite. Alder can't remember ever feeling this shaken, even with thousands on the card table. Everything feels surreal—like he's the target of one of those elaborate prank shows, lured into a setup.

His cabin appears ahead, tucked into a pocket of dense evergreens, the green shimmer of Goodwin's tail dancing over the roof.

All he wants now is to get inside, eat something, and hit the bed. He's got a twenty-four-hour shift starting at six a.m.

The Civic crunches to a stop at the end of the path, just to the left of the cabin. Alder shifts the car into park and sits there for a moment, eyes scanning the dark. The engine ticks and pings as it cools—each sound unnervingly loud against the stillness of the woods.

He leans back against the seat and rubs his face. Just get inside. Sleep. Then deal with the rest later.

The cold seeps through the window. Not sealed right. Thanks, Aubrey!

He exhales, watching his breath fog the glass before he finally reaches for the door handle.

He steps out. The night feels heavy, the kind of silence that presses against your ears. Somewhere in the trees, a pinecone falls. Then another. A soft clatter punctuating the stillness.

Alder walks toward the door.

A breeze kicks up, heard seconds before it's felt. Pinecones rain down—harder now—skittering across the ground, dancing under the green twilight.

The breeze brushes Alder's face. His nose threatens to run. He sniffs in the brisk, needling air.

Then it comes.

It starts distant, threading through the trees like a breath of wind. A howl—no, not a howl. Something else. Something wrong.

Like that bull elk's bugle, but warped. The pitch bends and twists, metallic and strained, like steel beams being torn apart, fiber by fiber.

An air-raid siren, smothered under grinding gears.

A painful cry, stretched and tortured, twisted into a wail no living thing should ever make.

Fifteen seconds, maybe more. Long enough to feel it vibrate in his chest, like the air itself is rattling against his body.

Then it cuts.

Silence.

A vacuum-tight silence. A stillness so absolute, it feels like something now lies waiting—listening.

A not-so-gentle suggestion shoots through Alder's amygdala. The rest of his brain scrambles to make sense of the bullshit out here.

He quickens his pace, fumbling with the key.

The lock clicks. He doesn't wait. He wedges himself through the gap, shoulder-first, twisting like someone evading gunfire.

He throws the deadbolt, slides the chain, and twists the secondary lock into place.

Chest heaving, he presses his back to the door.

Light floods the cabin as his trembling hand hits the switch.

"The hell was that?" he whispers, frozen in the center of the room, his voice barely audible over his pounding heartbeat.

"Aldi ... tha' hell is wrong with you, man? It's probably an owl or something."

The silence feels like a hogtie—leaving him vulnerable, waiting for the slaughter. Alder moves quickly to his old CD boombox, flips it on, and tosses in a Sister Nancy disc—a loaner from Mama Curlie.

"Bam Bam" thumps through the cabin, its rhythmic beat slicing through the stillness, but something feels off. The horns sound sharper, almost shrill, like they're tapping directly against his brain. The echoing lyrics. That droning horn in the background.

One by one, Alder flicks on every light switch, flooding the cabin with artificial brightness. Finally, he grabs the TV remote and turns on CNN. The screen stutters, freezes, and then sticks on a pixelated image of the female anchor, her expression distorted.

Satellite service has been unreliable ever since Comet Goodwin's sudden appearance three days ago, and its recent close pass has only made things worse. The comet's massive tail continues to disrupt transmissions.

At the bottom of the screen, the headline flickers and scrambles: *Comet Goodwin and—*

The image of the anchor's mouth held midspeech is frozen on one side, pixelated and flickering on the other.

The screen suddenly goes dark, followed by scrambled white letters and a choppy buzz for the Emergency Alert System.

It's cut off midbuzz. Alder doesn't get the alert message.

His chest tightens. *Breathe, Aldi!*

He flicks off the TV.

Too late. The frozen anchor, the droning alert—they're both seared into his brain. Every hair on his body prickles.

Sister Nancy's voice reverberates throughout the cabin.

Alder scrambles to the boombox and clumsily swaps the CD for a

Miles Davis disc. He skips to "All Blues."

This one still drones, but in a calming way, like the gentle hum of honeybees on a spring afternoon.

He plops into his easy chair and throws his head back. Even this position feels vulnerable.

Alder leans forward, and there it is—the framed photo of him opening a Christmas gift while his mother grins from the sofa. One of his favorites: a clear model of the human body. It took him weeks to meticulously build it, painting the arteries red and the veins blue. They streaked through the crystal-clear statue, catching the light as he turned it in his hands. He was so proud.

It hits like a boot kick to the gut. No warning. Guilt twists in his belly. He jerks his eyes away. If he can catch the tears before they collect, maybe he can outrun the storm.

Deep breaths. Four seconds in—hold four seconds—exhale for four—hold four—

Iiiiiin. Ouuuut. Rest and digest.

They're probably the same messages that have been blasting over the EAS: Remain Calm. Preserve all resources. They don't want folks running on the bank and buying up all of the toilet paper. As if, during a potential emergency, people would stock up on T.P., board up their windows, and shit the rest of their lives away. Ass hysteria.

Alder's functions sluggishly turn, starting with his grumbling stomach. It's begging to be fed.

Into the kitchen. Top Ramen it is. Side of broccoli. After that, sleep.

Later, while brushing his teeth, he studies his face in the mirror. He's still young—thirty-nine—but every night, his reflection looks older than the one before.

The job isn't even that hard, if he's being honest with himself. But it's not the work that's aging him.

It's the past.

It's the running.

When can I rest?

The Comet?

Comin' fort' to carry me home?

* * *

Alder's alarm blares at five a.m. He'd tossed and turned all night, sleep a fleeting luxury.

Groggy but determined, he jumps into the shower, gets dressed, and steps out into the brisk predawn air. This time, he remembers his coat and gloves.

His breath escapes in white plumes, curling into the icy nineteen-degree air. The Civic groans awake, its engine sluggish in the cold. The chill seeps into his gloves.

Something about predawn darkness—it's heavier, stranger than the night itself.

The car radio hums to life, tuned to Bart Ellis and "Behold a Dark Horse." The radio waves have been spotty, but less affected than the satellite TV transmissions.

Bart is mid-monologue. "… So, folks, don't always believe everything you're told … In fact, don't believe anything … not until you've proven it for yourself. Remember … lies grow bigger with less information given. They are inversely proportional."

Alder hits the CD button and slides in a disc Sharpie-marked "Mix #7." The first song: Beastie Boys' "Intergalactic." Perfect choice to jumpstart the day. Perfect song, period. Especially that buzzy, otherworldly robot voice droning on in its strange, rhythmic chant. It speaks to something deeper, something just out of reach—for those that can hear it.

As the Civic finally shakes off its chill, Alder pulls onto Gunmetal

Road. Comet Goodwin hasn't yet risen in the northeast, but its tail blazes across the sky, an unearthly streak of light cutting through the predawn stillness.

Arriving at Morningstar Falls Medical Center feels different this morning. The county sheriff's car is parked out front, alongside the hospital's only ambulance—MS1.

Inside, Alder finds Dr. Jennings already shrugging on his coat, ready to leave. One of the four patient rooms is occupied; the others sit eerily empty. The small staff—all three of them: two techs and Faith—are gathered around the occupied bed. Faith glances back at Alder, her expression tight with concern.

Jennings, with his signature suspenders, looks paradoxically calm away from the ruckus. He's ready to sign out and leave ... not get involved with that loitering.

"Morning, P-shooter ... Sheriff found a kid wandering out there. Seven years old. Strange case ... all yours."

Alder grabs the chart on his way to Bed 4. Jennifer Doe, it reads. The fluorescent lights flicker faintly overhead—a constant irritant Jennings never bothers to address. When Alder reaches the bedside, dread ripples through him.

A tiny girl sits crosslegged on the bed, intently focused on a coloring book in her lap. Her small frame is caked in dried blood, a gruesome coat from head to toe. Alder's stomach twists as she looks up.

Her green eyes pierce through the terracotta cracks of dried blood on her face. She smiles, wide and unsettling, splitting the blood like fractured clay.

Bats—not butterflies—flutter in his stomach, a cold unease tightening his chest. He glances at Faith, discomfort etched plainly across her face. Sheriff Tom, standing nearby, meets Alder's gaze with a similar look of concern.

The girl reaches forward from the bed and leans into Alder,

wrapping her arms around him.

"Hey, doc." Sheriff Tom's voice is low, steady, but tinged with unease. He turns to the little girl and gestures toward the hallway. "I'm going to talk to the nice doctor, OK?"

Faith gently pries the girl's grip from Alder's waist, her movements careful but firm. The girl resists for a moment, her green eyes locked on Alder's, before finally letting go. Dried blood flakes onto his scrubs, leaving faint, rusty streaks.

Faith glances at Alder, her expression heavy with something unspoken. He follows the sheriff out, leaving Faith and the little girl alone in the room. The rest of the night crew have already left.

In the hallway, Sheriff Tom stops and turns to Alder, his face tight and drawn. "Doc, I don't know what to make of this. We found their cottage way out in the woods. A place none of us even knew was there." He rubs the back of his neck, his voice dropping lower. "The girl kept saying something ... about needing to 'find herself.'"

"The place was ... soaked in blood. No bodies. No remains. Nothing to explain it. Just blood. We're guessing it was from her parents. It's gotta be foul play."

Alder feels the world close in around him. "What the hell?"

"Yeah. That's not all." Sheriff Tom's tone tightens. "We have no records for the little one. No ID, no birth certificate—nothing. It's like she doesn't exist."

Alder frowns, a memory tugging at the edge of his mind. "Hang on."

He walks back into Bed 4 and pulls open the curtain, where Willow is still working through her coloring book. "Willow? Is your name Willow?"

Willow's face lights up, and she nods excitedly. "Yep! Willow Rose!"

Alder's jaw tightens. A flood of saliva pools under his tongue, followed by a wave of nausea. The familiarity is unmistakable, even with her face obscured by a crimson mask of blood.

Faith raises an eyebrow at Alder, her tone light but curious.

"You know her?"

"No … nah, it's just—it's a long story." Alder fumbles with his pen.

Faith puts on a forced smile. "O—K! Let's go have us a nice bath, and then Dr. P will give us a quick checkup, hmm?"

Alder interjects. "Faith? Isn't your shift almost over? I'm sure that—"

She cuts him off with a wave, her expression softening but still distant. "It's OK! I'm here now!"

Alder hesitates. "Aren't you back on tonight?"

Faith's voice falters slightly, but she keeps her composure. "I said it's quite alright." Her almond-shaped brown eyes glisten as she holds back tears. She tucks a strand of her dark brown bob behind her ear, her hand trembling slightly.

Willow tilts her head, gazing up at Faith. "It's OK. Don't cry … I like baths!"

Faith lets out a shaky laugh, wiping her eye quickly. "Oh, yeah! Well, shall we?" She collects herself.

She holds out her hand. Willow takes it eagerly and skips toward the bathroom.

*   *   *

As Alder performs his exam, Willow smiles. She grabs his stethoscope, placing it on her chest, then giggles. The sound pulls an unexpected laugh from Dr. P. He shakes his head and thinks to himself, *Little goof.*

When he presses on Willow's belly, she squirms and kicks her feet, giggling even harder. Faith stands off to the side, tilting her head and folding her hands. Her warm gaze is fixed on Alder.

"Welp, you're all in one piece." Alder hesitates. Dammit!

Lord knows what this little girl had to witness. Her mother was possibly hacked to pieces right in front of her.

"I'm—I'm sorry. I didn't mean—"

Willow giggles. "I'm not in one piece?"

Faith's face shifts from momentary concern to amusement, her chuckles joining with Willow's. The sound of Faith's calming laughter draws Alder's attention. Their eyes meet with that feather softness—the flutterbyes gather in a belly circle, ready to get down.

Maybe it's the relief of an awkward moment.

No, it's more than that.

Sheriff Tom's voice cuts through the tension, his boots visible at the bottom of the curtain. "Doc?"

Alder holds a reassuring smile for Willow, which he drops as he steps into the hallway. He scribbles in her chart: *No definitive injuries on head-to-toe exam. Patient denies abuse, laughs at appropriate moments. Smiling and interactive. No bruises, no bony tenderness or deformities,* yada yada yada.

"Yeah?" Alder replies to the Sheriff as he continues scribbling.

"Doc …" The sheriff hesitates, his tone low and serious, his brow furrowed. "We're going to have to call CPS on this. There's no record of a Willow Rose in the state. The name she gave for her mother? There are thousands of women—and a few men—with that name in the US, but none in this area. We'll need state PD's help to dig deeper."

A shiver runs down Alder's ribs. "You're sure?"

Sheriff Tom nods grimly. "It's like they don't exist. Hey, Doc, we will need to draw blood from her—send it down to the lab for a blood type so we can compare it to the scene. Would that be OK?"

"OK. We'll get it. Then what's next?" Alder asks.

"Well, we'll take her into custody until the CPS worker gets up here. With this snowstorm rolling in, that may not be for a few days."

Alder nods. "Well, I guess it's settled."

Faith pulls back the curtain and walks out, her arms wrapped around herself. She must be exhausted—three hours past her shift's end. "So, what's the verdict, gentlemen?"

"Sheriff Tom is taking her into custody until CPS gets here," Alder explains, then glances at the sheriff. "From there, they'll place her, right?"

The sheriff shrugs. "That's the plan."

Faith reenters the room and squats beside Willow's bed. Her voice is warm but strained. "Hey, beautiful. You're going to ride in a big ol' police car and hang out with the nice policemen! Doesn't that sound fun?"

Willow's face reddens; her eyes brim with tears. What's coming is obvious to all present.

She pleads with a thick voice, "Please, I'll be good—I promise!" Her voice cracks; tears pour down her red face. "I have to stay here!"

Faith tries to console her, but the words don't come. She looks to Alder, her eyes silently begging for help.

Alder steps in, his voice calm. "Hey, it's all gonna be OK. He's going to make sure you're safe! He can protect you. Nobody can hurt you with him around!"

"That's not true!" Willow sobs, her voice cracking. "I have to be with you! We have to stay together. Please, Dr. P … Don't make me go!"

Alder shakes his head. "Willow, you have to go with the police. We have to work here … and …"

"I'll be good, I promise! Please …" Willow's voice cracks with emotion. Her mouth trembles, and her wide green eyes sparkle through her tears. She drops her head, tucking her chin as her body quakes with silent sobs. Tears splash onto the white sheet, blooming into a dark stain.

Alder and Faith look at each other, then at Sheriff Tom, who steps away with his mouth pressed against his radio.

Faith asks, "So, what if she sticks around here today? Hopefully it won't be too busy, and then I'll be back at six p.m. to help. Would that be OK, Dr. P?"

Alder feels put on the spot, thrown off-guard by her tender, expectant eyes. He freezes and stammers nervously. He looks at Willow, and the huge weight of expectation and unexpected responsibility hits him. *I can barely take care of myself,* he thinks.

The heaviest weight, however, is from a surfaced memory of his father's unexpected death when he was around the same age. It's his most distant childhood memory. He can't bring himself to let this little one down.

Sheriff Tom returns. He rubs the back of his neck and signals to Alder that he needs to speak with him privately. Alder follows him into the corridor.

"I spoke with CPS downstate," Tom explains. "That snowstorm that blew past us has everything locked up down there. They're OK assigning temporary custody to you … if you're OK with that." He tugs at the sleeve of Alder's hoodie and pulls him farther into the hallway.

"I think it works out better for the kid right now, Doc. I know this is not protocol, but none of this is typical—I've never even dealt with a possible murder before. You don't have to agree to all of this, a'course."

Alder pinches the bridge of his nose. "Yo—hey, I'm not—" He sighs. "Oh, OK … sure." *What am I saying?* "Why not?"

Sheriff Tom puffs his cheeks, then blows the air out slowly.

"I know this isn't by the book, Doc, but CPS says, with the storm, this is our best option for now. I'll log it all officially—just in case anyone asks questions down the road."

Sheriff Tom steps away with his radio pressed against his lips again.

Willow, in earshot, springs off the stretcher, runs to Alder, and buries her face in his stomach, squeezing him tightly.

"OK," Alder says, patting her back awkwardly. "But try not to get in the way. If somebody really sick comes in, you have to behave."

"I promise I'll be good!" Willow throws her fist in the air triumphantly, her face lighting up with pure joy.

Faith glances over at Alder, a playful smirk tugging at her lips. It's that look again. Alder catches it, and, of course, his cheeks redden again.

Other than Willow, there are no patients. The hushed moment allows Alder's stomach to remind him of a harsh truth: he hasn't eaten much in days. Meal amnesia—an occupational hazard of twenty-four-hour shifts.

He tries to recall his last proper meal. Was it last night? Or the morning before? The details blur together, lost in the fog of snatched bites.

"So ... Willow, are you hungry?"

Willow nods emphatically, licking her lips playfully, like a cartoon dog. "Pancakes?"

"Yes, pleeease!" Willow says. Her stomach speaks as well, but with a lower-pitched reply.

Alder smirks and points. "Lemme guess. Blueberry?"

Willow twirls in a circle. She bounces on her tiptoes. Oversized orange hospital footies sag around her ankles.

Alder smiles. Blueberry pancakes are his favorite. His adoptive mother used to make them every Saturday. Willow has the look of a fellow blueberry pancake fiend.

He reaches into his pocket, then calls over to an ER tech who's gazing up at one of the suspended patient TVs.

"Vin?"

The tech swivels toward the central station, eyes flicking between Alder and the screen. "Heyo, Doc! Morning. This comet deal is crazy, right? Those crazy alerts about being calm ... ugh."

"Yeah—I, uh—my car got hit by one of the meteorites. Came off the tail, I think. Smashed my windshield and driver's side window. And I'm pretty sure I got robbed getting 'em fixed at that salvage garage up north on Gunmetal."

Vin sucks air through his teeth. "Yeah, Konrad's a crook, Doc! Coulda told you that. Miserable bastard, that guy."

Konrad, huh? Not Aubrey? Intentional troll behavior, I bet.

Alder's thoughts stall, flickering between the here and now and something deeper. *The sky is falling—shattered my windows, shattered this little girl's life. This feels familiar somehow.*

"Hey, Vin? You wanna grab breakfast at Miss Curlie's for the crew this morning? My treat. Have her fix a blueberry short stack for the kid."

Alder hands Vin his credit card.

"You got it, Doc. On it—lemme go around, grab everyone's orders."

Alder nods. It's not a huge purchase. The ED staff is small—two techs, two RNs for the first twelve hours, one night nurse for PM, and the doc. Other departments exist in this tiny critical access hospital, but the ED feels like its own world.

Faith gathers her bags, keeping an attentive, concerned eye on Alder—like she feels guilty for leaving.

"You'll be OK with this?" Her tone is light, but the worry in her eyes says more.

"Yeah, I mean, if it stays like this, should be no problem. I got Vin and Russ with me. Willow can use the call room for a nap if it gets crazy. CPS should be on the way anyway."

"OK … I'll see you tonight. Goodnight, Dr. P."

"Night. Be safe, seriously. The sky is literally falling."

Faith lifts an eyebrow, then nods. "I will. You too. You need more luck than I do—incoming!"

Willow airplane-runs past Alder and throws her arms around Faith. "Bye, Faith! Remember, you promised!"

Faith smiles, squeezing her tight. "I know, baby girl. If you're still here, there'll be chocolate-chip cookies with me."

Alder tips his forehead. "Try to get some sleep, Betty Crocker."

Faith smirks. "I'll get a few hours. See ya later, eh?"

Alder winks. He doesn't realize his gaze lingers on Faith as she leaves, the tension that's been there all along dialing up a few notches. Maybe he's been blind to something—until now.

He turns to find Willow watching him, grinning wide and clapping her hands together.

"I know something you don't know!"

"Oh yeah? What's that?"

Willow giggles and skips back to the hospital stretcher. She dives onto the bed, rolling onto her back with another burst of laughter, eyes on Russ, the other ER tech.

Russ stands bedside, arms folded, eyes on the TV. Her strawberry-blonde hair is tied back in a loose ponytail, and both pant legs are rolled up to show off her chunky rainbow socks. She's twenty-four, with tomboyish charm, a single nose ring, and a calm steadiness that makes her everyone's right hand. When there's a problem, she's got a solution.

Willow's eyes droop. From the central station, Alder watches as Russ drapes a pre-warmed blanket over her and switches off the TV.

She leans down, voice low. "Alright, pun'kin, time for a joke before sleep. Why don't skeletons put up a fight?"

Willow mumbles, "Whyyyy?"

Russ smirks, one brow arched. "Because they don't have the guts."

Willow bursts into giggles, her eyes wide with delight. Russ gives the blanket a final snug tuck.

"But you?" she says softly, brushing back a strand of Willow's hair. "You got plenty, pun'kin."

She slips out from behind the exam-room curtain and settles into a chair at the station, flipping open a dog-eared fantasy novel entitled *Gayle Wynd*. On the cover: a sword-wielding warrior woman in a resolute stance, with mountains towering behind her.

For now, Willow is the only customer in their *not crazy* shop. A pace they'd very much like to keep.

* * *

Watching the little blanket lump of Willow, Alder feels a twinge of something familiar again. She looks so cozy, nestled in her improvised haven, wielding that innate superpower kids have—coping with the world through simple comforts. It stirs a memory of a night long ago—wrapped in a hand-sewn quilt, on the last day he saw his father.

That July morning in 1974, his father, Tim Peony, had taken him to Funtown, a now-defunct amusement park on Chicago's Southside, at 95th and Stony Island Avenue. Alder had begged to go every time the jingle played on the radio.

Alder was seven. He remembers the laughter. The two of them pumping up and down on opposite sides of a hand-cranked railcar. "Inspiration Information" by Shuggie Otis rising and falling in his ears as they rolled past the spaced-out park loudspeakers.

His dad's afro bobbed with each pump—a small, endearing detail that Alder clings to even now. He had a way of making Alder laugh, right up until that moment.

The metal screeched with every turn of the crank, and the thick summer air carried the mingled scents of popcorn, cotton candy, and hot pavement.

Toward the end of the track, Tim's laughter stopped abruptly. His smile vanished, replaced by a grim expression—a look that burned itself into Alder's memory. Years later, he saw that same expression during his first year of residency: the face of the first patient to crash in front of him.

When the railcar stopped, Tim swiftly scooped Alder up and gently set him on the ground. A moment later, he collapsed, clutching his left shoulder—his body splashed onto the pavement, the sharp click of his teeth breaking against it sending a shudder through Alder.

The open air felt like an endless tunnel to him. The stares of other kids, one holding a dripping ice-cream cone—all of it sticking to his jaw like the mumps.

"Oh, bless his lil' heart!" a woman muttered, her voice like glass cutting through the choir of onlookers.

Clown-head cutouts lined the walkways, their unsettling grins adding to the gallery of gawkers.

The Shuggie Otis song faded, giving way to the cheerful yet tinny Funtown jingle, drifting on a weak breeze from a distant loudspeaker.

That tune still lingers in Alder's memory—a jangly, retro guitar riff and tambourine, straight out of the seventies, now a nauseating clash of sound. The chorus voices add to the horror of the song, in that moment. The song that once beckoned him to the amusement park, turned on its head.

Timothy Peony died that afternoon. Later that night, Alder found himself in a Catholic group home, a sterile place that smelled like candle wax and old oil soap.

Alder remembers curling in his bunk, cold despite the heavy summer air. He had never felt so alone or scared.

Then, feeling a comforting warmth wrapped around him. A sister with kind eyes draped a hand-sewn quilt over him, fresh from the dryer.

His dad did the same thing on cold nights. He remembers its sense of cozy safety. The familiar scent—just like home—how it became the only stable thing in a now uncertain world. How did she know? The same scent?

Alder liked to think his dad told her—sent her a message from beyond. She was a sister, after all. Sisters could do that.

A single woman, Nina Graham—Mama—the only mother he's ever known, adopted him a month later. She gave him everything he needed to become the man he is now: a burned-out, debt-ridden, single, thirty-nine-year-old emergency physician.

He wishes he could see her again. He'd settle for just one missed hour at her bedside. But he can't. She's gone.

Alder shakes off the memory and turns his attention back to Willow. She looks so peaceful under her blanket, her small frame relaxed and still.

Vic returns with food from Miss Curlie's Diner. Russ rouses from her reading. She slides her paperback onto the counter and places her Gameboy Color inside to hold the page.

The aroma of sweet and savory goodness fills the station, causing Alder's stomach to growl in hunger.

Vic dips his head into the room. "Should I wake up Willow, Doc?"

"Nah," Alder replies. "Let her rest a bit longer. We can warm it up later—she's gotta be exhausted."

The crew unpack the paper bags, pulling out Styrofoam containers that send waves of warmth into the air. Suddenly, a small hand appears at Russ's side, tugging at her scrubs, followed by Willow's sleepy face peeking around her waist. She wipes her eyes with a tiny fist and tugs at one of her sagging hospital footies, a drowsy grin spreading across her face.

Alder shakes his head with an affectionate roll of his eyes. "Hungry?"

The adults exchange smiles, falling into an unspoken rhythm. Together, they set up a spot for Willow at the station—effortless, like they've done this a hundred times before.

Russ stacks a few basins, padding them with towels, over and under, crafting a makeshift booster seat. The MacGyver of ER techs— resourceful, always right on time.

She taps the seat then lifts Willow up with ease. "Up we go, pun'kin."

Willow raises her arms to allow Russ to lift her up and over into her breakfast perch. She sits facing the counter, looking over the food, smiling.

A quiet camaraderie settles over the group as they present Willow with a simple comfort amid her superheroine strength— warm blueberry pancakes. Russ ensures Willow is steady and able to participate, checking on her often.

Alder opens his container of pancakes. On top, a handwritten note: 'For Aldi. Love you, Mama Curlie. P.S. Tell Faith to come by! It's been too long!"

*　*　*

Darkness.

A faint blue glow pierces through, revealing the cramped call room with its narrow bunk bed. Alder lies on his stomach, head turned, one eye squinting at the screen of his Razr:

6:19 p.m. No missed calls. No messages.

The 'S' word is off-limits—its only acceptable use reserved for the mantra: Sleep when you can.

A rhythmic thumping sound seeps through the door, faint at first but unmistakable. It's coming from the main ER. Alder groans, rolling off the bed's edge.

The door creaks open, and the harsh fluorescent lights throb his eyes. The source of the sound becomes clear. Someone found his CD booklet. "Double Dutch Bus" by Frankie Smith blasts over the mini boombox speakers. This one is from his guilty-pleasure old-school discs. He burned it using a sketchy P2P program from an uploader named *ElectricSheep7*. Any song you want.

In the middle of the ER, Russ, Vin, Faith, and Roland dance in a loose circle. Their laughter echoes off the green walls, filling the space with pure, unbridled joy. The day nurses have already left, but Russ and Vin linger, staying behind to soak in the moment. A short, green, ghostlike figure bounces in the center of the circle.

Alder shakes his head, leaning out farther to confirm what he thinks he sees. Willow. She's fully dressed in an oversized green hooded sweatshirt—just like his. Hers is too big. Her hood shadows her face, and her blonde locks peek out around the neck.

Willow moves with carefree energy, arms pumping up and down to *raise the roof.* Her knobby knees bend in too-big jeans as she bounces. Russ dips in and grabs Willow's hands, swinging their arms side to side. Everyone's cackling, in complete hysterics. Faith braces her stomach with one hand, covers her grin with the other, laughter spilling through her fingers.

Not in the mood for their antics, Alder closes the door with a soft click, then flops back onto the mattress.

Where in tha' hell is CPS?

He shuts his eyes, determined to steal a few more minutes of rest. But the music's still thumping.

Then—

A flash. Just like when the meteorite struck.

Blinding. Soundless.

"What tha' rasshole!" Alder rasps.

He jolts upright, smashing his forehead against the bunk's metal grate.

Pain explodes across his skull, triggering a second flare of light behind his eyelids. His ears ring.

He rolls left, bracing himself on the narrow mattress. The flash fades. He waits for the window to blow out.

Nothing.

He grits his teeth, breath sharp.

No explosion follows.

Alder scrambles to his feet, stumbles to the door, and bursts into the ER.

Faith is sitting on the floor, cradling Willow in her lap. The girl trembles violently, her face buried against Faith's chest.

"What happened?" Alder shouts, scanning the room. "Did you see that?"

Russ answers. "We don't know what happened! She just fell and started trembling. She won't say a word … See what?"

"The flash—that light," Alder presses, looking around.

Russ's confused expression deepens. There are no windows in the main ER—if the light had come from outside, then they wouldn't have seen it.

Alder fixes his eyes on Willow, who still cowers on the floor.

Her head snaps up at the sound of his voice.

In an instant, she scrambles to her feet, runs to him, and throws her arms around his waist, clinging tightly. Her trembling melts into stillness.

She looks up—teary-eyed, desperate—and tugs hard at the hem of Alder's scrub top.

"Please … stay out here!" Her voice cracks. "Stay! Or it'll come back!"

Faith kneels in front of Willow, her voice soft, coaxing. "What, sweetie? What's coming back?"

Willow shakes her head, words spilling out, frantic.

"Don't leave! You gotta stay!" Her head shakes. "We have to stay together or everyone gets hurt!"

The oblivion—that's what makes Alder's blood run cold. What the hell is happening?

He clenches his jaw and, for a fleeting moment, considers jumping into his car and driving straight to Chicago with Blues Brothers haste. He'd even take Vegas and test his limited willpower over Morningstar Falls right now.

Alder swallows. His voice comes out low and uncertain. "Willow … W-what do you mean?"

Willow doesn't answer. Her small hands loosen their grip, and she steps back, climbing onto the makeshift booster seat by the counter. She grabs a slice of pizza from an open box. Faith must've brought it for dinner. Beside it, a craft-store bag full of clothing sits open, also presumably brought by Faith.

The girl's voice is small but steady as she says, "I wanted the hoodie like Dr. P's." She tugs at the green sweatshirt she's wearing, the same shade as Alder's, her head down as she nibbles at the pizza.

Faith approaches Alder, her arms folded tightly across her chest. Her gaze is intense, concerned, and searching his face for answers he doesn't have.

"Hey," she whispers. "Did you sleep OK? We didn't want to wake you. You never get this much sleep on shift. We figured you deserved your gray-cloud moment."

Alder chuckles weakly. "Thanks." His eyes drift back to Willow, her small figure so vulnerable in the oversized hoodie. His expression darkens. "So … y'all really didn't see that flash?"

Faith shakes her head. "No, nothing. You think it was another one of those meteorites? Vin told me about your accident. Did you get hurt?"

"Nah." Alder rubs the back of his neck. "I'm good. It shook me up a bit, though. All of this has me shaken up, actually. Something feels wrong, and I just … ugh."

Faith's brows knit together as her gaze flickers to Willow, then back to Alder. She hesitates before speaking again, her voice low and steady.

"Alder," she says, "you know you can talk to me. I'm out here alone too."

A loud, piercing scream erupts from the triage area. A woman's voice, raw with terror.

"Help! Help him! Please, God, somebody! Help!"

Alder and the entire crew sprint toward her.

Faith yells back toward the ER. "Willow, stay here, love. We'll be back. I promise! Roland, stay with her?"

Inside, a woman who looks to be in her thirties stands drenched in blood, her clothes clinging to her like a second skin. The metallic stench of iron saturates the air.

Her whole body trembles, her blood-smeared lips quivering as she struggles to speak. "Jake—m-my husband—my J-J-Jake—please—oh my GOD!" she stammers, her voice cracking, desperate and raw.

With a bloody, shaking hand, she raises her arm, pointing toward the glass doors. The chill of the breeze that followed her inside fades, replaced by an unnatural, suffocating warmth as the doors slide shut.

Alder's stomach bubbles as his eyes trace her trembling gesture. Terror climbs his neck like a panicked spider.

The ruby-red tint of blood, streaked in chaotic, panicked patterns, blurs the view beyond the glass.

Alder's inner self whispers: *Turn back. Hide. Call the sheriff. Let someone else deal with this. This is not sleep deprivation.*

"Shit—ah—shit—um," Alder stammers as the crew awaits his command. It's always on him to make the next call, and right now, he wishes this fell onto someone else.

He reaches for something deeper—stronger than terror.

Responsibility. Duty.

Instincts usually buried by fear.

Besides, running and hiding is something he's gotten used to over the years.

"Shit. Let's go!" Alder's voice cuts through the air—sharper than he intended.

Faith and Alder move first. Russ and Vin grab a stretcher from the wall and follow into the frigid night.

*   *   *

Snow flurries swirl beneath a darkened sky. The overhead lights in the parking lot are out, casting the area in eerie stillness. The glow from Goodwin's tail seeps through thickening clouds, casting a faint, widening light across the snow, heralding the storm to come. Meteor showers streak across the sky like paparazzi flashes, their glowing threads slicing through green and shadow.

There's no sign of the woman's husband.

No body. No movement. Only blood—a port-wine spray stretching across the one-acre lot, staining the snow in dark, violent streaks.

All is silent except for the whistling wind and the faint hiss of snowflakes dissolving against warm skin.

Then, the sound comes.

That same haunting sound Alder heard the other night.

A warped, metallic screech twisted with a primal, pain-laden scream.

It drags on longer this time, filled with malice. And yet beneath it, there's something else—raw pain and desperation.

As the sound fades, Alder's eyes catch a faint golden-orange glow deep within the forest beyond the hospital. The light flickers like a dying ember before stretching wide—gaping like the maw of some massive, unseen creature. Two blue flames flicker above it, like large, unblinking eyes.

For a moment, this image appears to rush toward them—the low bushes and shrubs bending forward from the motion—but just as quickly, it recoils back into the trees, swallowed by the dark.

Paralyzed by a rising chill, Alder stands and stares.

"Did y'all just—" he starts, voice unsteady.

Russ cuts him off, her voice brittle. "Yeah, Doc. We heard it. Creepy as hell!"

"No." Alder swallows, forcing calm. "I heard it too. But … did you see that out there?"

Everyone shakes their heads. Faith and Vin exchange uneasy glances toward the shadowed forest, but it's clear they haven't seen what Alder has. He realizes, with a cold certainty, he was the only one to witness the fiery glow—the monstrous maw closing in the distance.

Alder's circadian rhythm is destroyed, and he's exhausted. Regardless, he's having difficulty processing this one—he's writing it off like the meteorite incident.

"Everybody back inside. Now," Alder orders, his voice firm. "Russ, Vin, call the sheriff. Wait here until he arrives to escort you home."

Vin nods immediately. "You got it, doc."

Russ hesitates, trembling. "O-OK."

As the group moves, Alder casts one last glance toward the forest. The glow is gone, swallowed by the oppressive darkness. Yet the dread lingers, thick and suffocating.

Near the entrance, a small figure catches Alder's eye—Willow. She stands in the doorway of the ER, frozen, her eyes wide with terror.

Alder's breath catches. "Why is she—? Good lord."

Her sweatshirt hood slips back as Alder scoops her up, holding her close.

He feels it immediately, a prismatic warmth, tingling and sparking as it seeps into his body, deeper than he thought possible. Unseen tendrils latch onto his very core, pulling and clinging to his soul. It feels like euphoria-laced electricity darts into his chest. He feels strength, evident in Willow suddenly feeling weightless in his arms.

Her tiny body jolts, her fingers digging into his sweatshirt. Her eyes meet Alder's, silently searching for reassurance. He forces himself to appear calm, though tension coils through his frame.

Then the sound returns.

It feels closer this time, as if it is a presence right at his heels. The grating racket cuts off as the automatic doors slide shut with a dull thud, leaving only the crew's uneven breathing.

Alder sets Willow down gently, his arms trembling. Faith steps forward, pulling Willow into a hug. "It's OK, sweetie. You're OK. Everything's alright," she whispers, her eyes darting to Alder, searching for reassurance of her own. The rest of the team looks at him the same way.

As the strange sensation fades, its absence feels just as unnatural. Alder exhales, grounding himself as the weight of the moment presses down.

In the triage area, the crew spots the bloodied woman slumped against the wall, appearing catatonic. Roland is kneeling at her side, trying to calm her. The metallic tang of blood hangs heavy in the cramped twenty-by-twenty space.

Russ ushers Willow into the main ED, shielding her from the sight. Vin and Alder approach the woman cautiously, gloved hands ready. With Vin and Roland's help, she silently stands, her eyes closed and remaining that way for the rest of the night. She speaks to no one—not the crew, nor Sheriff Tom, who arrives moments later.

* * *

Alder examines the bloodied woman. Faith stays close, using her gift—her voice—to soothe her. Likely a new widow. Who knows?

She doesn't speak, but now she at least responds—nodding, shaking her head. A flicker of something human returning.

In the call room, a makeshift cave has appeared: blankets draped over the lower bunk bed, likely Russ's handiwork. She opted to stay overnight. Alder peeks inside to find her rainbow socks poking out from the blanket fortress. She and Willow's soft snores mingle in the hush of the room.

He leaves them both the room to rest. He slept all day anyway. He'll stay awake tonight.

Vin gets an escort home from Sheriff Tom.

After the woman's exam and a hot shower, she calms enough to speak with the in-house crisis worker. From there, a sheriff's deputy takes her into protective custody. She's not out of the woods. There'll be more questions ahead.

Outside, the snow thickens, but Sheriff Tom decides to patrol anyway. He seems determined to get to the bottom of both strange cases: Willow's missing mother and Jake, the man whose blood still paints the parking lot in long, arterial streaks.

A creeping uneasiness settles over Alder. It feels like something is right behind him, squeezing both shoulders—waiting to pounce.

The icy wind howls, forcing its way into the ED with each opening of the doors. Snowdrifts trigger the motion sensors, leaving Alder no choice but to turn them off and lock the doors. EMS will radio in if needed. Considering the night's events, this feels like the safest option.

CHAPTER THREE

In the aftermath of the earlier events, it's now *slow* and *quiet*.

Too *slow*. Too *quiet*.

Roland was sent home under Sheriff Tom's watch, leaving just Alder and Faith beneath the dim, humming fluorescent lights. They both sit at the central station.

The old TV mounted in the corner flickers, muted. The scrambled news ticker at the bottom moves too fast for Alder's tired eyes to track. He bobs his head absently—half to Al Green's "Love and Happiness" playing quietly from his boombox, half to the weight of sleep tugging at him. He sits facing the ambulance bay on purpose, feeling vulnerable with his back the other way.

Faith reads a paperback, *Glorious Escape*. After a while, she exhales through her nose, tucks her bookmark into the crease, and lays the book in her lap. Her foot taps the linoleum in a pokey, repetitive motion. She touches her parted lips with her fingertips. A moment's hesitation, then she speaks.

"So ... off-topic ... contract's almost up? I guess you'll be heading back to sweet home Chicago?"

Alder cuts in too soon.

"Yeah. Mmhm. Two more months. That's me."

He cringes slightly. *Not smooth!*

"Wow. You say that like you're in a hurry, eh?" Faith smirks.

There's something endearing in her voice, especially that soft Canadian accent curling around that little "eh." It always makes Alder smile, and tonight is no different, though his smile is nervous.

"Nah. It ain't like that. It's just ... no place like home, right?"

Faith looks down. Her fingers find the three-heart locket that hangs in the V-neck of her scrub top.

"Yeah, I guess." She shakes her head slightly. "You know ... I just realized how little I know about you after four months."

She looks at his left hand.

Alder chuckles. "Well, there isn't much to tell. What do you want to know?"

"So, is there a Mrs. P?"

Alder flushes. His demeanor flips as he tries to calm the shy-boy emergence by easing into a near-confidence. He's aware of the tension. At this point, it's no longer an assumption.

"Nah, I mean ... naaaah!" He shrugs his shoulders and tries to shoot her a debonair look with lifted eyebrows. "You?"

Faith's confidence seems to kick up a notch as well, as if she's just gotten the reassurance she needed as well. The energy changes in the room, flipping from ominous to communion. A wall was just knocked down, and they are standing on either side, facing each other.

Faith bites her lower lip, tilting her head. "No, not married. Not anymore, at least." She pauses. "No kids."

A flicker of something crosses her face—a microfrown, then a knowing smirk.

Alder snickers. "No kids? With all that baking?"

Faith giggles, cheeks flushing. She pats the book on her lap, eyes dropping.

"Well ... I like to bake for others." A beat of silence. "For the smiles."

"The smiles?" Alder leans in.

"Yeah, the smiles." A shy grin spreads across her lips as she rolls her eyes playfully. "Baking is about the smiles. Sometimes, when I bake ... my cheeks hurt because I've been smiling the whole time."

She snickers. "Except for sourdough. Not too many smiles from that. I haven't mastered it yet."

Alder is intrigued. Faith has his full attention.

She continues, voice softer. "Then there's the smile when you …" She clears her throat. "When someone takes a bite." She blushes. "My smile. Theirs. I can feel their hearts in that moment. I live for that."

Alder shifts closer. Eyes locked. Leaning in.

"Hey, you wanna—"

The blaring alarm of the telemetry radio cuts him off. Morningstar Falls EMS is calling in.

Faith sighs and stands, pressing both palms into her temples as she walks to the radio. She pauses just before lifting the phone, takes a deep breath, then answers.

"Base Station."

The male voice crackles through the static. The signal is still patchy, thanks to Goodwin's appearance.

"Base Station—MS1 en route with a sixty-seven-year-old male, alert and oriented times one. Confused. He's burning up with a fever. Blood pressure is low—eighty palp—we can't get a full reading. IVs are in both ACs, two bags of point-nine wide open. ETA … uh, maybe twenty minutes? Visibility's down to one hundred feet—total white-out conditions."

Concern flickers across Faith's face. "Alright, guys. Keep the fluids running and start five mics of dopamine. And please, be careful out there. Tony, when you get here, stay sharp and watch your surroundings. I'll brief you both when you arrive."

"Ten-four, Faith. See you soon."

Faith sets the radio down and turns to Alder. "Sounds like we're getting Mr. Benoit—a nice older man. Ojibwe from near Morningstar Falls. He's got a bad prostate and gets UTIs because of it. A regular, though it's been a while." She pauses, glancing toward the door with a faint sigh. "Looks like tonight's the night, eh?"

*   *   *

The arrival of MS1 ambulance makes the ground shake slightly under their feet. Alder walks towards the bay doors and flicks the switch at the top to unlock them for the paramedics.

Both doors slide laterally, and cold air assaults Alder. Snowflakes follow, melting and leaving small drops of moisture on his face.

The ambulance beeps as it backs toward the door to a stop. The brake lights redden both Alder's and Faith's faces. A short female medic leaps down from the driver's seat onto the snowy pavement and trudges through the gray slush.

"Hey, Faith. Doc P."

Faith reaches out and pops open the rear of the ambulance, where Tony, the other medic, steps out with his clipboard.

"Hey, Doc. Faith! You know Mr. Benoit … a sixty-seven-year old male—"

Faith cuts him off. "It's OK, Tony. We know Mr. Benoit. Hi, sir, it's been a while. What's going on?"

Mr. Benoit rambles incoherently as the medics pull him out of the rig. The legs of his stretcher fall to the ground and plant into the two inches of accumulated snow. His gray-streaked hair is in a ponytail.

Mr. Benoit grimaces. "Ohhh—that hurts … my back is on a wild ride."

He looks at Alder. "… and there was a man … he was very dark and on a mission to get here."

The man's body starts to shiver violently. "He's altered," Faith says as she pulls his blanket over his neck. "Let's get him inside, eh."

They quietly roll Mr. Benoit into Bed One, away from the call room to avoid waking Willow and Russ.

Mr. Benoit mumbles, "Two trees grow roots deep into the firm earth— they share—they share—they grow—they tear down the … wind—"

Alder walks beside the stretcher, unwrapping the blankets. Mr.

Benoit is wearing Ojibwe necklaces and stones.

Alder smiles. "Boozhoo, Mr. Benoit."

"Aaniin!" Mr. Benoit replies with a smile, a twinkle of coherence creeping into his eyes. "You … can call me John."

Alder shrugs. "Sorry, Mr. Benoit, I'm old-school—it's a respect thing—but you can call me Alder. How are you feeling?"

"My back. It's on a mission—to fulfill … stay together." Mr. Benoit's eyes flutter.

Alder turns to Faith. "He's burning up—delirium. Let's get some fluids in him. Antibiotics. Six-fifty of tramadol? Grab a urine dip?"

Faith nods gently as she slips between the bed and Alder, facing him. "Of course, Doctor. And a six-fifty of Tylenol."

"Sorry—Tylenol, yeah. Scatterbrained. Sleeping, but not well, you know?"

She places a soft hand on his shoulder, one silken auburn brow arched. "I knew what you meant."

Then she pulls away—subtle, sudden—her eyes flicking down as a flush rises to her cheeks.

Alder feels it again—that pleasant, butterfly-inducing tension. She smells good. She always does. Lavender and vanilla, the perfect scent for night shifts.

Their eyes meet beneath the flickering fluorescents, and for a moment, everything stills. When Alder realizes how close they are, warmth creeps up the back of his neck, flooding his face.

It's more than attraction. When she touches him—even by accident—it's like a live current passes between them, looping back, surging stronger with each return.

His gaze drops to her badge.

Faith Linden, R.N. Caring since 2002.

Linden. Soft, steady, dependable eyes—that hold sadness.

He flicks his gaze from the still photo to the real thing—tonight they're brighter. More alive than the image clipped to her chest. They peer back into his, and her head tilts.

Alder stutters. "Um—heh, y-yeah—Tramad—Tylenol."

He clears his throat.

The tension between them is the only thing keeping his brain from slipping into full-blown panic. Because lately, he's been teetering on a ledge.

He feels that something is watching.

Stalking and waiting.

Waiting to swoop in and snatch him by the throat.

That comet is a part of it. He doesn't know how, but he feels it deeply and undeniably. Stronger than paranoia.

Back to Faith. He's noticed her before, sure, but now something about her feels grounding—stabilizing—like a buoy in a vast, uncharted ocean. He wants to hold onto her. But he knows he'd only drag her down with him.

The medics exchange a glance, smirking slightly, eyes widening in silent amusement.

Tony, the medic in charge, heads out of the room and says playfully, tapping Mr. Benoit's shin, "Take care, John—of yourself and these two!"

The other medic snickers and carries the empty stretcher back, her footsteps squeaking in the eerie silence as she walks away. The ambulance bay doors slam open, and the smell of exhaust rushes in.

Alder's pulse spikes. The wind howls. He moves behind Tony and pats his shoulder.

"H-hey, Tony ... be careful out there. Something crazy is going on. Maybe a madman or something stalking about. Please—watch your backs!"

Tony winks. "Thanks, Doc. You too." He snickers.

A strange sound—like the one from the other night, only farther off, hooks Alder's ear. Tony doesn't react.

Wheeeeeeaaaaaaaarrr—

It cuts out as the bay doors thud shut in front of him.

Behind Alder, Mr. Benoit's monitor beeps steadily. From the central station, Taana Gardner's "Heartbeat" thrums softly from his mini boombox.

Alder reaches up, shuts off the automatic door, and locks it with a soft, final click.

* * *

Over the next few hours, Alder and Faith work to stabilize Mr. Benoit, who becomes more coherent as his blood pressure and fever normalize.

5:00 a.m.

Alder walks to his bedside.

"Morning, Mr. Benoit. You're lookin' better," Alder raises a thumb. "Your fever's down, and you look about ready to run a marathon—but we'll skip that for a few days. In the meantime, we'll get you and your luggage up to the presidential suite soon."

John snickers, wincing from a stitch in his side. "Thanks, Doctor. I knew it was coming on too. Haven't been able to piss for two days—just filling up to the brim. Damn prostate. I get these infections, and they climb up to my kidneys." He grunts. "Feels like somebody took a bat to my back."

Alder continues, "So, about last night, do you remember anything?"

"No, not really."

"Something about the roots of a tree?"

"Oh yeah, that I do remember." John sits up in bed, groaning. "I'm from a lineage of seers. I get visions." He turns onto his side guardedly, as if sudden movements are painful. "We get visions all the time, especially when we detach from the physical body or are close to death. For me, it's these damned urine infections."

John chuckles, but the laughter is cut short by a grimace. "Ugh, shit—my kidneys! Doc, can I get some of the good stuff?"

Alder nods. "Of course. I'll get you some Ketorolac. That'll take the edge off."

He continues, eyeing John curiously, "A seer? These visions ... at least last night, you had a really high fever. Delirium is the most likely—"

Mr. Benoit shakes his head and interrupts with a raised hand. "I must've been about ready to check outta here, because that vision was as bright as day! The trees were connected, almost as if they were sharing the same roots across long distances." He shakes his head. "I don't know what it means. I just know what I see. It has meaning. Maybe it's for you to figure out."

Alder squints, a twinge of skepticism flickering across his face—but beneath it, he's intrigued. The man's seemingly incoherent psychobabble feels important. There's something there, buried.

He double-takes, then turns out of the room.

At the central station, Faith is watching him. A dazed smile lingers on her face. Then, as if startled, she blinks, straightens, and pretends to rifle through her pockets, eyes flicking downward.

* * *

Russ and Willow emerge from the call room, both yawning. As a floor orderly wheels Mr. Benoit from the ED to his room, he catches sight of Willow and points at her, his expression shifting to one of sudden awareness.

"Remember!" he says, his voice lowering and filled with an odd certainty. "Goodness, I think that fever's back, Doc." He falls back in bed, his cackling more unsettling, as if something unseen is fueling it. His eyes narrow at Willow.

He's wheeled away. The sound of his throaty laugh lingers, echoing down the hall like a pinball being slapped back and forth.

Faith grins and kneels to Willow's level. "Morning, nugget!"

"Good morning!" Willow says, rubbing her eyes and smiling.

Faith takes Willow's hand and leads her into the bathroom to clean her up. She brought changes of clothes with her the previous night at the start of the shift. Though they fit Willow, they appear to have belonged to a little boy. Willow clings to the muted green hooded sweatshirt that matches Alder's.

There's now a car booster seat on the counter, next to a sack stuffed with clothes. Faith's hands linger over the clothing, her movement freezing for just a moment before she continues.

Alder walks to check on Russ. "You think you'll make it through the shift? I'll talk to Nurse Anna, maybe she can get by with one tech today."

"I think I'm good," Russ replies. "I can't believe how fast I passed out—slept pretty decent."

After a short while, Faith brings the washed-up, brushed, and dressed Willow out of the bathroom. The little girl bounces with a grin on her face. She runs up to Alder and grabs his hand. "I'm ready!"

Alder is taken aback. "Wo-ho-oah!"

Faith shakes her head slightly. "Oh no, no. We forgot to phone Sheriff Tom and CPS. Let's do that. They should've called by now."

Willow skips around Alder joyously. He feels a sense of impending discomfort—one that will have him taking guardianship of little Willow because CPS is still stranded, and she doesn't want to go with anyone else. That feeling is sealed when he sees Faith's face as she slowly puts down the phone.

"I just spoke with Tom's deputy," she says. Her voice is steady, but her eyes flicker nervously. She pauses. "CPS did call, and they won't be here until the roads are cleared—likely not until later tonight—tomorrow, even."

"Oh?" Alder replies, unease forming a pit in his stomach.

Faith continues, concern stretching across her face. "The deputy said he lost contact with the sheriff last night. He hasn't answered his phone, and he hasn't made it home."

Alder's impending sense of discomfort deepens into an impending sense of doom. An uncanny chill makes the hair on his neck rise. Something is wrong—something is coming.

He glances down at Willow, then over at Faith, who appears to be waiting for a response.

"Can she go with you? I mean—it's a little girl and—you're a girl."

Faith's smile wavers slightly as she reassures Willow, but there's a flicker of something else in her eyes—something Alder can't quite place. "Of course. That would be perfect. We'll have so much fun. Right, Willow?"

Willow's eyes widen in terror, and her small hands grip Alder's arm desperately, her fingers digging into his skin. She trembles, pulling herself even closer to him as her voice cracks, "No—please—we can't! I have to stay with Dr. P, always!"

Alder realizes that, legally, this little girl was placed into his custody. It doesn't matter that he thought this would only last for the shift. He feels the tug of familiarity, pulled back to the time of his father's death, when he was left in that group home. How small and afraid he felt. How he wished there had been someone he could trust the way Willow trusts him now.

He sighs, the weight of the moment pressing down on him. "You knew to bring a booster seat?"

Faith replies, "Well, I realized she's small for a seven-year-old. I knew it'd be a miracle for CPS to make it up after that storm. I felt we couldn't leave her here, so I was prepared to volunteer." Faith giggles lightly. "Seems her mind is made up, eh?"

Alder shakes his head. "Apparently. So, what do I do now?" His question is laced with both humor and sincerity.

Willow's eyes brighten, and her small hands stretch toward the sky as she beams up at Alder. "Blueberry pancakes!" she bellows, her voice full of excitement.

Faith smiles. "I could eat. May I join?"

Alder lifts his brow. "Of course. Miss Curlie's, I guess? My treat?"

Faith giggles. "I got this one! I'll follow you guys in my car. Let me warm it up first?"

Alder is exhausted, but running out the clock until CPS arrives doesn't sound like the worst idea.

Shaking off messed-up stuff goes along with working in an ER, and it's often done over breakfast for night-shifters.

CHAPTER FOUR

6:45 a.m.

The two cars pull up in front of Miss Curlie's Diner, a small joint tucked into the sea of pines along Gunmetal Road.

Mama Curlie stands outside, a shovel planted in the snow as she surveys her work. Her face, reddened by the cold, is wrapped in a scarf tied like a babushka, and her tiny mouth stretches into a smile as she spots the cars.

In the sky above, Comet Goodwin rises. Appearing slightly smaller than the moon, it glows pale white, its tail stretching southwest.

The comet rises alongside the sun, visible in the northeast as the sun climbs in the southeast. As the day progresses, the comet's tail arcs slightly northward, always pointing away from the sun as it itself moves southeast to southwest. Like a painted sundial in the sky.

Every time Alder sees the blazing orb, he's overcome by a sense of doom. *It's here for me.*

Faith steps out of her worn 2001 Toyota Sienna minivan and waves. The moment Mama Curlie sees her, she clasps her hands with joy.

"Faith? My goodness … It's been too long!" Mama Curlie calls out as she strides toward Faith, arms open for a hug.

Faith says, "Hi, Miss Curlie!'

At seventy-five, Mama Curlie is spry, moving with the ease of someone half her age. She squeezes Faith tight, then rises on her tiptoes to kiss her forehead.

"Come on in. Let me feed my babies. Hi, Aldi!" she says, her tone casual but affectionate as she turns to Alder, her more frequent customer.

Alder smirks. "Morning, Mama Curlie."

She's the only person who calls him Aldi, other than his adoptive mother.

Willow unbuckles her seatbelt, and Alder holds her door open as she hops out.

"Oh my goodness ... and who is this princess?"

"Willow!" she exclaims with a bright smile.

"Willow? So pretty! And your favorite iiiiis ... blueberry pancakes?"

Willow's eyes go wide in amazement. "Wow! You're magic!"

Mama Curlie grins and taps her temple. "Mama Curlie knows, dear heart. Let's go!"

She takes Willow by the hand, and as they walk, she playfully taps Faith on the lower back, winking at her. Faith blushes. Neither of them realizes that Alder caught the exchange.

Inside, the diner is eccentrically but tastefully arranged. Booths line the windows, their seats worn yet welcoming, bathed in the glow of dim, honey-colored light. Mama Curlie has always been a traveling woman, as she likes to say. Originally from the south, she moved to northern Minnesota after being swept off her feet by her late husband. She calls herself a reverse snowbird.

She loves reggae, and her old jukebox holds many classic records. "Shark Attack" by Wailing Souls is playing when the trio enters.

Alder stiffens. Something about this song—its ominous bassline, the lyrics—he can't pinpoint it, but it sends a shiver through him. It feels like a warning—a whispering of some looming truth, just beyond his grasp.

Pictures from Mama Curlie's travels with her husband cover the walls, arranged seemingly haphazardly. They filled any open gap with newer pictures as soon as space opened up, creating a vibrant collage of their adventures. Someone had drawn a mustache on a picture of Mama Curlie mounted on a horse, grinning widely—only she knew she had done it herself.

The aroma of comforting goodness lingers in the air, wrapping the diner in warmth. From behind the counter, the sound of sizzling drifts out. Mama Curlie's attentive cook works the griddle, flipping breakfast for a couple waiting at the counter. His head bobs up through the kitchen window now and then, scanning order tickets.

Beyond them, the diner sits mostly empty due to the snowstorm, with most of the town busy digging out.

Willow perks up the moment she spots two old-school arcade machines—Mortal Kombat and Donkey Kong. Her eyes lock onto Donkey Kong. Bloodcurdling screams and punching sound effects ring out of the former, while Donkey Kong plays in demo mode silently.

"Jumpman! Can I play? Please?"

Alder digs in his hoodie pockets, searching for quarters. He pulls out a handful from his left pocket, the metal jingling in his palm, and hands five to Willow.

"Here. We'll order the pancakes. Only Donkey Kong—not the other game!"

Willow glances at the game titles, then shrugs. "Donkey Kong? The name's wrong—it's Jumpman! My da—"

She stops herself, appearing confused, as if she's lost her train of thought.

Alder and Faith exchange a glance, smiling. Alder catches Willow staring, her mouth parted as if she wants to say something, but she just tosses her coat aside and skips toward the arcade machines. Before the coat even hits the floor, Alder snatches it—only to realize it's not hers.

A red Mighty Morphin Power Rangers puffer coat. A boy's coat.

He exhales, shaking his head as he drapes it neatly over the seat.

They settle into a middle booth as Mama Curlie sheds her scarf and coat, revealing an array of beaded necklaces and earrings. Beneath her cardigan, she wears a vibrant, dashiki-style tunic, its colors deep and rich against the warmth of the diner's dim lighting. Round glasses frame her kind, baby-blue eyes, and her curly silver hair gleams in the glow of the overhead fixtures. Her voice is sweet and reassuring, the kind that makes you feel like everything is just as it should be.

Alder and Faith pull off their coats but keep their heads on a swivel, both of them watching Willow from less than fifteen feet away. Her small body jerks from side to side as she maneuvers Jumpman up the ladders, dodging barrels with surprising precision.

Alder leans in slightly, eyes narrowing. A seven-year-old this good at Donkey Kong? That piques his curiosity.

He glances left. The jukebox hums, framed by a glowing green rim. "Shark Attack" plays, its muffled pulse filling the quiet diner. The warm orange glow at its center—the place where the needle drops—draws his focus. He can't help it. It reminds him of that mouth, splayed open last night.

His gaze flicks forward. Faith is watching him. Their eyes meet, holding for what feels like minutes. A weight lingers between them, unspoken.

Alder clears his throat, breaking the silence.

"So, tired?"

"No, I'm OK. I don't sleep much. Maybe five hours or so. I have a hard time living alone and all. After last night, not sure I'd be able to sleep anyhow."

A microfrown flashes across Alder's face. He feels that there's more beneath this, something deeper.

"Have you always had that problem … with sleep, I mean?"

Faith hesitates, and her expression shifts. Her eyes reveal the weight of something she's been carrying.

"My last relationship was … abusive." Faith rolls her eyes. "An understatement if there ever was one."

Alder sits forward, caught off guard by the sudden shift. The words land like a gut punch. He's always sensed there was something more to Faith, but not this. He wants to say something—anything—but words of comfort don't come, just more questions.

"Abusive? Are you safe?"

Faith laughs, but there's a rawness to it, and threatened tears give it a thick sound in the back of her throat.

Alder fails to hide the shock on his face.

She exhales. "He's locked away. Prison. I won't have to worry about him for another twenty years or so."

"Prison?"

She looks down. "Yeah ... attempted murder and manslaughter." Her hands cross over her pelvis.

Alder's stomach tightens. She says it like a passing fact, but nothing about this is casual.

"Shit. I'm sorry. Faith, I didn't mean to—"

"It's OK, it's OK!" She wipes a tear just as it falls, her hand shaking slightly as she stares at the table.

"He wanted children, and I couldn't give him any ... I lost the first one. That's when the beatings started. The choking. The—"

Her voice thins. She stops. Swallows.

"My body was his."

She snivels softly, her voice breaking as her eyes fill with tears.

"The second pregnancy was the worst. It was like somebody turned the dial up. I barely survived." A shuddering breath. "It was a boy."

Alder leans back, processing it all. In just a few minutes, he has learned more about Faith than he has about most other people in years.

Faith continues, her voice low. "I couldn't get pregnant after that. They had to take my uterus to save me."

She grips her glass and takes a long sip, as if the water could wash the words down.

"We got the son he wanted eventually. A foster son, but when the abuse turned to him, he was taken away. Just as we were about to adopt him. I protected him ..." Faith's voice wavers " ... the best I could ... When I couldn't, I turned the bastard in … and I lost my boy because of it."

Her fingers tighten around her glass. "They wouldn't place a child in an abusive home, right?" She sniffles. "But that's OK, right? We're both safe now. He's with his loving family—eight years old and happy. And I'm here. I slipped across the border."

Alder leans in. "Canada? Is that where you're from?" His voice is soft. "Is that why you're way out here? In the middle of nowhere?"

Faith gives a single quick nod. "Yeah. Being a nurse made it easy to cross the border and get permanent residency."

Alder's gaze drops to her necklace. A locket.

"Your locket … Is that for your three—"

He reaches toward it—just a small movement, unconscious—but Faith jumps.

Alder freezes. The shift in her body is instant—shoulders up, throat tight.

He quickly pulls back—hands up, palms open. "I'm so sorry, Faith. I didn't even think."

She exhales sharply, shaking her head. "It's OK. It's OK. I just get a little jumpy around my neck, that's all. Just because …"

Her voice falters. She wipes the corner of her eye, her breath catching.

Alder sees it now—the weight she carries. The loneliness of hiding from a past that nearly swallowed her whole. A life spent trying, failing, suffering. A life spent in the shadow of a narcissistic monster. Neglecting her own needs just to keep the peace.

Instead of tenderness, she knew fists. Choking hands. Hands that didn't comfort, they crushed. Hands that didn't hold, they suffocated.

Escape wasn't a choice.

Now, she bakes muffins, searching for the smiles she's long been denied. She takes occasional trips to the craft store in the city, but mostly, she stays put.

Willow bounces into the booth next to Alder, her oversized green hood flopping over her face. She shoves it back with a quick motion, flashing her radiant smile. She's out of quarters but doesn't seem to mind.

As she settles in, Mama Curlie approaches, balancing stacks of steaming blueberry pancakes and warm syrup. The rising steam curls in the air, like tiny ballerinas dancing atop blue-jeweled hills. Her cook follows with more breakfast and a pitcher of Mama Curlie's special papaya drink—Alder's favorite. It tickles his jaw, sweet at the tip of the tongue, the perfect balance to the fluffy hotcakes.

Mama Curlie glances at Faith, something knowing in her gaze. As if she heard the conversation without needing to. As if she's always understood. Faith must have confided in her once—maybe in words, maybe in silence.

* * *

Bob Marley's "Sun is Shining" crackles to life on the jukebox. A better song? Maybe. Alder thinks, hopes. No. It doesn't feel like it. The lazy scat, calling out each day of the week, drapes over the diner like a fog. Saturday. The melody drones, settling too well into the moment, into his skin.

Between the lulls, he hears it again—that awful, banshee-like shriek. The gaping maw in the clearing.

Alder has not *shaken off* the events of last night. He tried, but they fizz at the edge of his mind. Just enough to make the uneasiness linger.

And then, hearing Faith's voice break. The weight of her past. It burns in his gut, like coals in a furnace. The bastard's rotting in prison, but Alder still wants to drag him into the snow—make him feel every ounce of what he did with his own hands.

And then there's the comet. A flickering, sedately moving eye—watching everything. Its tail drags behind it, a nightly promise to return. Three days now, and still no one knows how long it'll stay.

The *effing comet.*

Alder's restless appetite swings back and forth.

Faith sits with an excited posture as she cuts Willow's short stack into neat, bite-sized pieces. The knife softly scrapes the plate with each cut as Willow bounces in her seat, fork in hand, eager to tear in.

Alder's stomach knots, then grumbles. He exhales, then sticks his fork into a stack of pancakes, layering them onto his plate. The steam rises, sweet and buttery, curling into his nose.

Appetite's back.

If he ever had to choose a last meal, this might be it.

* * *

Willow, Faith, and Alder finish their pancake breakfast while Mama Curlie watches from behind the counter, smiling. Of course, when it comes time to pay, there won't be a check. She refuses to take money from Alder. He'll try to insist. It won't fly.

Faith stands first, helping Willow shimmy into her coat. They giggle the whole time.

Alder rises, unable to hide his own smile. Breakfast hit the spot, and Willow's silliness is infectious. At one point, she had picked up two forks, pretended two squares of cut pancakes were feet, and stomped them across her plate like a long-legged dinosaur, complete with tiny, growly roars.

Mama Curlie follows them out to the car, pulling Alder aside as Faith helps Willow into the backseat.

Faith leans into the car, still talking with Willow, doting on her in a way that makes Alder pause. He hasn't seen her smile like this—not in the four months he's known her. She lights up with Willow, and that alone casts a radiant glow around her beauty, affecting Alder in a way he can't explain.

Alder lingers, pleasantly lost in watching them for a moment—until he turns and finds Mama Curlie watching him, watching all of them. She smiles, one brow raised.

"She'd sure hate to see you go, Aldi ... Me too."

"I'm gonna miss you too, Mama Curlie. I'm serious—you've made it tolerable for me here. And who do ya mean? Faith?"

"She always talks about you."

Alder blushes.

"Me tellin' yuh true, Aldi ... dat woman head-gone fi you."

She giggles. So does he.

He has always loved the way Mama Curlie occasionally flips into patois. She looks like your typical adorable white granny, but Jamaica is her favorite place on earth, and she even talks the talk here and there. She only does it with him, never a lick with anyone else. It's their little thing, and it always gives them both a chuckle. And while patois is different than his mother's Bajan Creole, it still brings him comfort.

"I don't know about all of that ..." Alder looks back at Faith. "Really?"

Mama Curlie silently gives a single, sure nod.

Alder continues, "Nah."

Mama Curlie grabs Alder's shoulders and squares his body in front of hers. Alder towers over her at six feet two, but she has a presence that stretches beyond her small stature.

"You are allowed to be happy. Everyone is. The pain comes when a person doesn't feel they deserve it. It's yours to have. Toss those other thoughts away with your fears and other garbage. Be happy ..."

A dull pressure builds behind Alder's eyes. Today, those words hit hard. Mama Curlie always knows the right thing to say, and he really is going to miss her.

"Aldi. You two are going to be OK. I promise this with every bone in my body!"

Alder agrees, gazes down at his toes. "OK, Mama Curlie. I hope you're right."

"I am. Now, go get some sleep, dear heart. I love you both."

* * *

Faith and Alder stand facing each other, their breath making white plumes with every word spoken. After a short while, Willow falls asleep in her booster seat in the back of Alder's car, and time seems to slip away as they talk outside Miss Curlie's diner.

"You got this, Dr. P. I mean, Aldi!" Faith giggles.

Alder smirks and raises an eyebrow. "We got jokes, I see."

"Yeah. Plenty of jokes." She pauses, her tone turning a little somber. "It does feel like a joke sometimes, doesn't it?"

Alder, sensing where she's going with this, responds, "Life? Yeah ... more than we care to admit."

Faith shifts uncomfortably. "By the way, I'm sorry for sharing too much earlier. It's just that—"

Alder cuts her off, offering a gentle smile. "It's OK. I'm glad you opened up." He meets her gaze. "You're a beautiful soul, Faith. I wish I'd gotten to know you sooner. Who knows, the contract might've left a better taste in my mouth."

Faith tilts her head, her cheeks reddening as she looks down nervously. Alder glances around, and once he sees they're unwatched, he softly reaches for her hand.

"I'm not sure if I'm off-base here, but ... would you like to go out sometime? Just the two of us?"

Before he finishes, Faith nods eagerly. "Yeah! I'd—" She snickers bashfully. "Yeah! I—" She stops again, laughing at herself. "God, I sound desperate. I swear I'm not. I just ... like you. A lot. I was hoping you'd ask." She shrugs. "But you seemed so ... private."

Alder nods. "I tend to be, but the loneliness out here trumps my desire to be a recluse. I could've used a friend."

He winks at Faith, who blushes.

She looks at her watch and exhales. "I'd better get some sleep. Unlike you two, I'm back on tonight. You got my number. Call if you need me."

Alder feels that uncomfortable sense of impending doom again, and like before, he struggles to pinpoint where it's coming from. Is it the fact that he's a Black man now responsible for a little white girl in the middle of nowhere? The overall sense of doom tied to the events of the last few nights underscores that feeling.

"See you later?" Alder says, his tone taking on a fatalistic edge.

He gets into the driver's seat and tilts the mirror to see Willow's neck leaning to the left, fast asleep. Maybe she'll stay this way. He hopes.

He turns the key.

"Intergalactic" blasts through his speakers. Alder fumbles with the volume, twists it counterclockwise.

He mouths, "Shit!"

Looking through the rearview, Willow's green eyes are smiling back.

"Sorry, too loud."

"I like that," she says.

"Sure, yeah. Of course."

Alder shakes his head and chuckles, then twists the dial back up.

Willow tilts her head side to side, her shoulders rocking to the buzzy robot voice. *Can you hear it?*

* * *

Comet Goodwin blazes in the upper right of Alder's vision, but he has a distraction. He catches himself bobbing along with Willow—it's infectious.

The robot chant finishes the song, and Alder turns down the volume before the next song queues. Willow stops moving in the mirror. She cackles and covers her mouth.

Alder shakes his head.

"Willow, I'm sorry about your mom." He pauses.

Her face becomes gloomy.

Alder squints slightly. He feels pressure behind his eyes.

"I, um … I lost my mom too." He nervously rubs the side of his neck. "Yeah, not too long ago … tssh … and my dad too, yeah. But that was a long time ago."

Willow diverts her eyes out the window, tracing her finger on the glass.

Alder continues, "I lost two mothers, I guess. I never knew my biological—you know, my actual mother. But my Ma … she died not too long ago."

Alder gazes at his eyes in the mirror and scrambles to catch the tears collecting at the edges. His eyes flick over to Willow's reflection, and she's wiping tears away herself as she peers out of the window. Her little lips are curled and trembling.

Something shifts in Alder. It's as if someone shook him, and a few books came off the shelves and fell open.

Alder Peony is not open. Most of his books are wired shut, by pain and/or shame.

"Hey, it's gonna be alright, yeah?" He glances over his shoulder, eyes flicking across the empty road. "I'm OK. You're gonna be OK too. Believe that. You believe that?"

Willow wipes her red cheek and nods. "Yes," she says, her voice thick.

Alder turns back. He didn't expect that deluge of tears just now. At least he's distracted from the existential dread of that effin' comet. He feels himself approaching a wave of catharsis, until Willow mumbles.

"She wasn't my real mom either."

Alder's eyes widen. "You were adopted?"

"Adopted?" Willow shrugs. "Is that when you lose your family and you get a new one?"

Alder shakes his head slightly, then nods. "Something like that."

Willow shrugs then nods, returning his paradoxical gesture.

"Yeah. I guess adopted."

Alder raises an eyebrow. He reaches for his cellphone and goes to dial Sheriff Tom. It rings once.

Beep beep.

The call drops.

Getting a signal out here is bad enough anyway, but the comet has made it worse. Calls barely go through. Alder has had no one to call, so it hasn't mattered. Until now.

* * *

Alder and Willow arrive at his cabin. He steps out of the car first. By the time he rounds the vehicle to open Willow's door, she's already unbuckled herself and wriggled free from the booster seat—perched on the edge, ready to jump. She launches herself out of the car before he can even offer a hand.

Willow waits as Alder retrieves the clothes Faith packed for her—a sizable care package, even pajamas. They're a little too big, but they're hers now.

She darts up the porch stairs, as if already familiar with them. Of course, she is familiar from her prior late-night visit.

She stamps down both feet by the door, then bounces on her toes. Alder is afraid that this is going to be a long day. His exhaustion is creeping back up. She's a live wire, and he's barely functioning.

With a sigh, Alder slides the key into the lock and pushes the door open. Silence. Darkness. He still has his blackout shades drawn. The scent of the cedar-built cabin spills out to greet them.

Alder reaches inside to flick on the light, and the cabin fills with a warm glow. Willow dashes in without hesitation.

Alder scrubs a hand down his face. "What the hell am I going to do all day?" he mutters under his breath.

"Do you have any games?" Willow asks.

Alder looks around. "I got cards. Yeah, cards." He shrugs.

Those cards are usually for him to practice counting, something he doesn't plan on teaching a seven-year-old. Even though he had learned when he was just a little older than Willow.

His mother's brother, Uncle Shem, who rarely presented for a visit, taught him everything he knew. Alder, being himself, wanted to master it—and that he did. He made stacks of money by gaming the system in Las Vegas, Jersey, or anywhere else he could find a casino. He could rack up thousands a night on the tables. Not anymore, and he definitely wouldn't be teaching Willow.

"Have you ever played solitaire?" Alder asks.

Willow wrinkles her nose. "Do you know any other games?"

"I Declare War? You know that one?"

She shakes her head.

"I'll teach you. It's fun. Easy." He grabs his keys. "Let me run to the car. I'll be right back."

When he returns, Alder discovers Willow patiently awaiting him, crosslegged on the front-room bear rug.

"O-kay!" Alder shakes his head.

Across from Willow, he opens a deck of cards, his fingers moving smoothly and expertly. "So—I'll show you how to play. Then, I guess we'll see." His eyes flick to the rustic clock on the wall; it's nine a.m.

This is going to be a long day.

Willow looks toward the kitchen.

"Do you have fruit snacks?"

Alder's lips curl into a half smile.

"Are you kidding? Of course. I got the good stuff—the kind that doesn't even stick to the package."

He chuckles, hops up, and heads into the kitchen. He tosses a pack to

Willow, who catches them effortlessly. Alder then grabs a second pack for himself and plops down in front of Willow. He deals out the first hand.

A few rounds in, she starts to pick up the game up. They go back and forth, neither backing down.

Mid hand, Alder gets a flicker of unease.

"Willow, do you remember being adopted?"

She shrugs. "I don't remember a lot. It's like dreams, maybe—I don't know." She shifts slightly, ruffling the cards in her tiny hands.

Alder's unease lingers, but he doesn't press.

Time for a break. It's an even split, five wins each.

"Dr. P, do you know any other card games? What about back-jack?"

"Blackjack?" He raises his eyebrows. "Nah, you're still a bit too young for that, kiddo."

Alder scans the room and spots a comic book—*Superman*. He hands it to her.

"Here, Superman! I'll be right back. I just need to step outside for a second."

Willow brightens, excitedly grabbing the comic.

"Oh … Ultra guy?"

Alder raises an eyebrow. "Yeah, sure. Ultra … Guy? Is that Superman's Dollar-Store knockoff or something?"

Whatever—he's got bigger concerns.

He dials the hospital on the way out, doing a double-take before one final glance back—she's engaged with the comic. He presses the call button as the door clicks closed, hoping to get Sheriff Tom on the line.

The bitter breeze whistles in the earpiece of his Razr cell phone.

Booop.

Call failed.

"Shit."

Alder tries again. Nothing.

"Of course."

He exhales, tilting his head up toward the sky. Don't look northeast. Don't look northeast. The last thing he needs is a status-panic spell while in this reverse Diff'rent Strokes situation. One of his favorite childhood shows back in the day. Don't ask what he's thinking 'bout.

Alder's gaze involuntarily traces along the tail.

No!

To the Nor' East.

Dammit!

Knots his guts every … single … time.

Alder takes a deep breath, then whispers to himself, "That was then. This is now."

Another deep breath. He exhales out. "That's up there. I'm down here."

Goodwin's tail is also the source of the heaviest meteor showers ever recorded. Because the tail is so close, the sustained showers are visible even in daylight.

One annoying thing is the temporary central blindness that comes with accidentally looking directly at one of the blazing meteors. They leave lingering, lilac-licked, lopsided, little floaters in your peepers. Purple is the word.

Alder thinks Willow is waxing and wide awake, while he is waning and withering.

He collects himself. Takes some more deep, cleansing breaths. His sponsors, plural, would be proud.

Play cards. Feed her. At some point today, CPS will call, and things will be back to normal. The plan.

Time for the act. Alder puts on a contrived expression of excitement before opening the cabin door.

"Alright. Next game. I'm not letting you wi—"

Willow is out cold. Curled in a tiny ball on the bed. While he was outside trying to get a call through, she had changed into pajamas from Faith's care package of clothes and climbed into bed.

Alder looks at the ceiling, wiping his hand over his face.

"Thank something!"

The Superman book is neatly on the bedside table, and the cards have been gathered and put into the card box, which she stood on its side. Alder has had a habit of doing that since childhood. Sort of a compulsive habit.

Willow's red Power Rangers puffer coat rests beside her. Alder picks up a throw from his easy chair and drapes it over her. He carefully plucks the coat from the bed and hangs it on the coat rack by the front door.

Mid-motion, he stills. His fingers linger on the fabric, his eyes fixed. Faith was a lifesaver for bringing these clothes. He exhales, about to let it go—until a sudden realization makes his heart sink.

These weren't just any clothes. They must've been for the son she couldn't keep.

Alder turns to look back at Willow sleeping. Her fingers twitch. Her lips part, whispering something he doesn't catch, but it makes the hairs on his arms rise. As if she's remembering something familiar to him. Something lost.

*   *   *

Willow sleeps most of the day, giving Alder a chance to steal a few splintered catnaps himself.

He rests in his recliner, while the immense space of the queen-sized bed swallows Willow's tiny body—each inch adorably covered by the peaceful animation of her sleep.

At one point, he wakes to find her sleeping upside down—with one leg propped against the headboard. Half-awake and disoriented, he lets out a soft chuckle and sinks back into sleep.

5:45 p.m.

Alder's Razr rings.

He never took the time to change the piercing ringtone from the default. It jars him awake.

Before he can answer, it stops ringing. No missed calls. No caller ID. It didn't ring long enough to log either.

Willow still appears to be asleep. Alder, still groggy, quickly dozes off again. Why not?

6:10 p.m.

Alder opens his eyes to find Willow trying to climb into the easy chair with him, her green eyes wide in her panicked face.

"Hey—hey—what's wrong?" he asks, his voice a mix of concern and confusion.

Willow doesn't answer, only claws at him, desperate to get into the safety of his arms. She's shaking, her breath coming in panicked gasps.

A knock at the door makes Alder's heart skip a beat.

Tap … tap … tap … tap.

The unnerving space between each knock builds a sense of deep dread, suggesting something unnatural will stand there with an uncanny grin once the door is opened.

"Yeah? Who's there?" Alder calls out, trying to calm Willow, who continues to climb into his lap, trembling with fear.

"Hey! Hold on, hold on!"

Alder lets down the easy chair and trudges to the door, but before he reaches it, Willow retreats to the farthest corner in the cabin. She curls into herself, her face buried into her bent knees.

Alder looks through the peephole and sees the silhouette of an ushanka hat. As the figure moves to knock again, the shimmer of a six-point star glints in the dim light—sending a wave of relief through him.

"Sheriff Tom?" Alder calls, his voice tight with both hope and hesitation.

The silhouette nods—tense, scanning the darkness behind him.

"Thank God," Alder breathes, unlocking the door.

Frigid air rushes in, stinging his nose.

"Evening, Doc P. Willow's here, right?" Sheriff Tom asks, his tone grave.

"Of course! Everything OK?"

Tom rests a hand on the doorknob, eyes heavy. "You'd better come out here for a minute," he murmurs.

Alder grabs his coat from the hook and slides into his slippers. The two men step out into the evening cold.

"Doc, something's going on," Sheriff Tom says, exhaling hard.

"I've noticed. Did you find placement for Willow?"

Tom rubs the back of his neck. "No. And now we can't even reach the CPS worker. We can't get a call outta here, and the radios are down too."

He lowers his voice. "We've found remains—bits of people, Doc. Scattered all over Morningstar Falls. Whatever did this … it didn't leave enough to identify."

Sheriff Tom pauses, his jaw tight. "Plain old foul play doesn't cover it. And Clara—her so-called mother—her blood came back O negative. But with Willow …"

He hesitates.

"They couldn't type it. Said it was untypeable. Maybe a lab error, or the blood broke down in the tube or something? Only thing … the DNA test was wonky too. Everyone has a blood type though, right, Doc?"

Tom releases a pursed-lip exhalation.

"My theory: Clara was some lonely transient who happened upon Willow—maybe she's got amnesia. Repressed trauma. Poor thing. We'll get to the bottom of this, I promise."

He sighs. "We'll need another sample. I've been trying to get through to the state police, FBI, anyone, but right now …"

He meets Alder's eyes.

"For her safety, I will need to take over cust—"

Before he finishes his thought, a sharp crack echoes from the woods, freezing both men in place.

Alder feels it like a warning under his skin, an eldritch prickle that crawls up his spine. A silent exchange passes between them as their eyes lock.

Then, the sound moves—quick, erratic—scrambling over pinecones and closing in fast.

A jittering noise emerges, growing louder, closer—quicker. Out of the corner of Alder's eye, he sees a flicker of golden-orange light skimming just above the snow.

Something scrapes the low-hanging pine branches, making them recoil—as if the forest itself feared what was coming through.

Alder turns, his breath pausing as he sees a massive set of antlers jutting from something wrong. It isn't an elk. It isn't a moose. Its eyes burn with a flickering blue glow, like cold flames in the dark. Its mouth stretches impossibly wide, revealing a seething pool of orange light, which causes its widely spaced, sharp teeth to glint.

Those screams he heard before. Now they are close and in surround-sound.

Sheriff Tom pulls his weapon and takes aim. The thing suddenly halts ... about ten feet away, kicking dirty snow into the air at them. Its flaming blue eyes snap about in their sockets as it rears up, towering over seven or eight feet. It stands up, remaining unnervingly still. Except, its broad torso is covered in slick, silent, snakelike appendages that slither in and out of its flesh.

There it stands. A hellish, foul-smelling statue. The stench is an assault on its own: rust, rotting carcass, and citrus.

Alder gags, and as he does, Tom fires a shot—but the bullet hits the monster with a whispered thud, like a nickel thrown into jelly. The creature doesn't react, and Tom's eyes widen in disbelief.

The *thing* remains still, its flaming eyes roving between them, lingering on Alder the longest.

Tom tightens his grip on the revolver. He clenches his jaw and pulls the trigger again.

Pop.

Nothing.

In a blur of motion, the monster blitzes. The sheriff doesn't have time to react, or even yell out, as the thing's massive jaws clamp down with a meaty thud, completely engulfing Tom's shoulder and upper arm.

The sharp, brutal snap of Tom's shoulder dislocating pierces the air. Tendons tear like thick rubber bands under violent strain. Then comes the crunch—the wet, meaty sound of ribs and upper arm being crushed. The sheer gore turns Alder's stomach.

His calves tense, as if massive hands are squeezing them and holding him in place. He teeters on the edge of consciousness.

His vision narrows to a dark tunnel, and at the end of it, the only thing his brain registers is the harrowing sight of Tom's assault.

Tom can't move. His head turns, eyes wide—as if taking in one last view of the world—as his own body is torn apart below.

He can't even scream.

Instinct screams at Alder to run, but his feet betray him. He stumbles backward and crashes into the snow, landing hard.

He sits there. Frozen. Helpless. A forced audience to this soul-crushing nightmare.

The creature's jaws clamp down, crushing deeper into Tom's chest. More ribs crack. His back jerks violently, swaying—his spine likely fractured.

Tom's mouth gapes in a silent scream. His body convulses, his collapsed lungs fighting to take a breath.

Just one.

A sip of air.

Enough to cry out.

Or at least say his final word.

As the creature decapitates Sheriff Tom, a crimson geyser erupts from his neck, spraying high into the night—shimmering like ruby shavings beneath the comet glow. His keys—once opening every door in his life, including the chest holding his coin collection—tumble to the ground as his frayed belt loop gives way. He used to visit the ER every day, always bragging about some new coin he'd added to that cherished collection.

The monster's gaze remains fixed on Alder throughout with an unnervingly intense look. A silent promise. *You're next.*

As the creature finishes its horrific feast, it leaves nothing behind but splashes of blood in the snow and across Sheriff Tom's car.

Then it twitches, its body jerking unnaturally as its head snaps toward Alder.

Its front end and face are drenched in the sheriff's blood, deep red and glistening ... until the blood begins to sink in, slipping between the snaking, headless serpents that cover its body.

The serpentine appendages move in a rhythm so fluid it's almost sickening—an undulating dance of flesh against flesh. They slither over one another, caressing the creature's body like a nest of thick worms.

Tom's blood seeps into the pit, forming pink bubbles on the surface. Each bubble pops into a stringy droplet, rolling downward—none wasted. Even that is swallowed by the creature's slick, gray, snakelike hide.

Alder, still on the ground, scrambles backward, willing his fear-frozen limbs to move—to try and stand. Then, a thought cuts through the panic.

Willow.

She's inside. Alone.

No.

She's just outside the door. Watching everything unfold.

She looks so small. So helpless in her oversized Star Wars pajamas.

Willow takes a hesitant step forward. Stops.

Then tries again.

Like she's trying to get to him.

Like her little body could actually help.

The monster's head jerks toward her, tilts.

Then snaps back to Alder.

Then back to Willow, as it stands between Alder and the cabin.

Alder scats in panicked bursts. "No! Willow—get—go—get—aahhh—"

The pain, the loss, the horror. Alder's decades of issues are nothing compared to what Willow has endured in just the last three days.

Enough.

Alder's legs tremble as he forces himself upright, pulling from a strength beyond himself.

And he runs. Not away, but straight past the creature, still fixed on Willow, long enough for Alder to gain a few feet.

Behind him—a click, followed by rhythmic thumping.

The creature gallops, then picks up, speedily closing in on Alder. He dares not turn around. His feet have never shuffled with such haste.

As he reaches the door, Alder frantically scoops Willow into his arms in a single motion. As he does, a deep warmth floods through his body.

It feels familiar.

It feels safe.

The bliss tugs at something buried deep. A memory: His father's sure arms carrying him through the dark. Laying him gently into the soft comfort of his bed. Wrapping him in warmth. A moment of peace—before sleep.

At some point, the creature must have lost ground, or maybe given up the chase. There's now a noticeable gap between them.

Alder bursts into the cabin, slamming the door behind him. Just as it's about to close, he sees it: a wide, glowing mouth filled with gnashing, knife-like teeth. Melted droplets weep from the icicles hanging off its antlers. Grotesque eyeless eels form a tangled mass across its chest and body. Its foul odor trails in after Alder, wafting into the cabin.

Outside the door, the creature emits a shrill, wavering screech.

Seized by a grotesque spasm, it arches violently, its limbs snapping erect as if pulled by unseen hands. It teeters for a breathless moment— then, with a sickening crack, it drops back onto all fours, turns, and vanishes into the pines. The underbrush thrashes violently in its wake.

A blinding light builds outside of the cabin. Alder flinches, instinctively shielding Willow.

The walls are consumed, the drawn shades bleached by the growing light. Static crackles in the air as the cabin groans and shifts around them. Alder's ears are filled with the sound of his own pulse. Squinting against the glare, his voice is choked with disbelief and horror.

The light plunges away quicker than it appeared. A dead silence swallows the cabin. Then, without warning …

Glass explodes inward, shards knifing through the air, clattering into the kitchen sink, and embedding in the walls. The screech of shattering glass rakes near Alder's ears. Cold night air rushes in.

Alder crouches against the door, Willow locked in his arms, both of them barely breathing. The dark silence is suffocating—leaving a sense of being bound. Even the hum of the cabin's electricity is gone.

Willow shivers. She's not wearing a coat. Just a pair of slightly oversized Anakin Skywalker pajamas.

"Dr. P—"

Alder shivers too, but not from the cold—from teeth-chattering fear. Willow's breath quickens, her trembling more violent than his.

Alder tries to reassure her despite his own fear.

"It's OK. It's OK."

He digs in, lifting her into a secure hold.

Willow's tiny breathless voice escapes. "Doc-t-or P …"

Alder doesn't realize he's gripping too tightly until she exhales a small, shaky breath against his shoulder. His hold loosens, yet his hands remain clumsy and heavy.

A sudden pop—and the refrigerator hums back to life. The lamps flicker on, struggling for a second before settling into a steady, warm glow. The darkness is gone, but a frigid wind blasts the cabin, pouring through the broken windows on all four sides.

Alder moves to the bed and sets Willow down on it. He's still, his gaze searching the room as he tries to determine their next move. They need to leave, but he's terrified of walking out there. What it just did to Tom—it's on repeat, flashing before his eyes, as if it happened inside of the cabin. His ribs stitch. He can't breathe.

Don't be a snivelin' rasshole, Aldi! Get it together.

In for four seconds. Out for four.

Alder grabs Willow's coat. Reaching into the cloth bag Faith sent, he pulls out a pair of jeans and a blue Winnipeg Jets sweatshirt.

"Get dressed. Quick like!" His voice is tight with panic.

Fear flickers across Willow's face as she stares up at him. Wide-eyed uncertainty replaces her previous composure. In a low voice, she says, "OK! Quick like!"

Jumping from the bed, she puts on the jeans and sweatshirt over her pajamas. Her oversized pullover sleeves conceal her hands, and her long pants trail on the floor.

Alder crouches, rolling up the cuffs of both legs, his heart clenching at the thought of Faith having to give up the little boy who once wore them.

He tugs her coat over her shoulders, then pulls a skullcap snug over her head. Faith had thought of everything. Finally, Alder snatches the nightstick from beside the front door.

CHAPTER FIVE

Alder cracks the door. He holds Willow protectively behind him as he peers through the narrow opening. He nudges it open a few more inches, just enough to stick out his forehead and his eyes.

Who-whooo.

An owl flaps its wings and vocalizes, launching Alder's body into fight-or-flight mode.

He snaps his head back inside, slamming the door shut. His pulse kicks up.

"C'mon, Aldi—get yo shit together, man!" he chants under his breath. He sticks his head back through, exhales sharply, then gently tugs Willow's puffer coat, pulling her close. He hustles them toward the Civic, twenty feet away on the path to the right side of the cabin.

Sheriff Tom's car blocks him in. Forest to the left. Cabin to the right. No clean escape. He scans around for the sheriff's keys, lost somewhere in the crystal snow. No time … he'll have to drive tight against the house, loop around the rear, then cut back onto the path. Not easy. Pines line the way.

Alder and Willow move quickly but quietly, stopping once. They pause. Listen. The air feels off—too still.

At the passenger door, Alder reaches for the handle. Carefully.

The door squeaks loud enough to make him grimace. His heart thumps. His head bobs with it. He lifts Willow into the booster seat, clicks her belt into place. Then, with measured motion, he eases the door shut. The sensation of something looming behind him builds.

It's in his head. Has to be. Still, he moves quicker.

He rounds the front of the car and reaches the driver's door—

Whirrrrrrrrrrrrrrr-aaaaaaawwwwwwwww.

The scream sounds far away.

He jumps in, slams the door shut behind him, and hears a crunch. His foot lands in shattered glass. The driver's window is gone. So is the rear driver's side. The windshield holds, but the cold air surges in, needling his skin.

"Mothafu—"

He stops himself, turning back to find Willow's emerald eyes staring at him.

The banshee screech rises, closing in.

Alder jams the key in. Twists hard.

A closer, louder screech rings through him—but it's not the creature. It's the engine. Choking. Failing.

"Motherfucker!" Willow blurts out, loud and clear.

Alder's head snaps up. In the mirror, Willow's green eyes stare back, then she bursts into giggles, hands over her mouth. He shakes his head and twists the key again.

This time the engine catches. Roaring to life.

"Hey, we don't repeat no bad words, OK?"

Alder cringes at the thought of sounding like his mother. He yanks the wheel and jerks the Civic forward, peeling around the back of the cabin. Branches whip his shoulder through the broken window. He leans right, dodging them, but never stops listening for the creature— footsteps, breathing.

Willow's head is craned to the left window, watching as broken pine needles and twigs spray into the car. She leans to touch them as they land on the seat, but they're just out of reach—so she sits back and watches them collect.

Alder clears the cabin. They're around the front when something catches his eye. Sheriff Tom's revolver. It glints faintly on the ground.

Alder hits the brakes, scanning frantically before flinging the door open. He sprints, grabs the gun, and stumbles just as his hand reaches for the car door.

"Are you OK, Dr. P?" Willow's voice floats through the shattered windows.

Alder pushes up, steadies himself. "Get it together, Aldi," he mutters under his breath.

"I'm good. Quiet down now," he says in as normal a voice as he can manage.

He springs up and into the car, slams the door shut, and throws the Civic into drive. Tires grind against the dirt. He peels off, whipping past Sheriff Tom's car, then tears down the path.

He swings onto Gunmetal Road.

Five miles to Morningstar Falls Hospital.

Above them, Comet Goodwin's fanned-out tail flickers, like lightning that has been imprisoned within the clouds.

*　　*　　*

Cold air rips through the broken window as Alder barrels along at seventy-seven miles per hour, heading for the medical center.

He flips open his Razr with his chin and speed-dials the hospital. All he gets is a busy signal.

"Shit," he grunts.

A bright light washes out the sky, blinding him. Willow buries her face in her sleeve.

"Cot-dammit!" Alder yells out. It's silent otherwise, just blinding brightness. He slams his foot down on the brakes.

The motion of the car coming to a roaring stop overtakes Willow and Alder, yanking them forward against their seatbelts. A loud snap rings out from the bottom of the car, followed by a shrill grinding sound.

He can't see anything but the outlines of blue pines burned into his retina. The vehicle veers to the left.

The light dies down.

"It's gonna happen … down! NOW, Willow!" Alder commands, expecting an explosion to follow, just like that one morning. He whips round and fumbles with Willow's buckle, yanking it free. Then he throws himself over the seats, shielding her tiny body with his. He feels it again, like a shared current, electric … not just from the slap of fear—this is different.

Alder holds his breath. Waits.

Nothing.

No explosion. No impact. Just silence.

Then … Willow's voice, soft and steady. "It's OK, Dr. P. We're OK."

He looks around nervously.

All is in its place. No carnivorous monsters. No meteorites.

"Heh! It's all good. Heh."

Willow nods softly. She too scans the surroundings, her eyes wide and cautious.

Except the car is dead—and everything's gone dark.

Click—

"Get down!" Alder ducks as the lights of the vehicle turn on. He uncovers his head and sits up, then helps Willow back into her seat. "OK. Let's get out of here."

He slides out of the rear driver's side door—and stops cold.

The car is leaning left, off-kilter.

His stomach knots. Something's wrong.

Alder steps out. The front driver's side passenger wheel—gone. Not just flat. Snapped clean off the axle.

Behind Alder in the car, a tiny fist raps on the window. Willow has scooted to the window.

"Dr. P, I have to pee!"

"Hold on—just hold it."

Her innocent eyes look at him with a slight sense of desperation.

"Really bad!" she pleads, bouncing in her seat.

A lot has happened tonight, and neither of them have managed to take care of their basic needs.

"Shi—" Alder catches himself. "OK … c'mon. Out here. If I tell you to run and get in, I need you to do just that. Run inside, hit the floor, curl up—get small, invisible."

"OK! I promise. I'll do good."

Alder scans the area. Trees line the road, their dark silhouettes pressing in. Beyond them, dense boreal forest.

He sucks his teeth, shakes his head, exhales a choppy breath.

"OK … over there. I'm coming with you. I'll turn my back."

"Dr. P, stay close. We have to stick together, always."

Alder shakes his head, barely listening. "Yeah," he mutters.

The untouched snow sparkles under Goodwin's tail, glimmering like scattered green diamonds. For a moment, it almost looks magical.

Willow wanders a few steps ahead, scanning the woods, her diminutive body barely making a sound as she moves—just the faintest sound of snow packing under her feet.

She stops near a clearing between two pines, where the trees pull inward like ribs—their trunks packed too close, their branches laced together overhead. A tight space. Smothering. Alder doesn't like it.

Still, it's private. Probably a good hiding spot.

"Over there," he says, nodding toward the area. "I'll be right here, looking that way. Just be quick and watch around you. Willow? Do you understand?"

"Yes. I know, Dr. P. I promise to do good."

She scans around slowly, trying to find a spot with a discriminating search, similar to a poodle finding a wee spot. Her head turns side to side, then back at Alder.

She points to a sparse collection of trees, which appears private for her, but nerve-racking for Alder. It's only feet from where they are standing, but he can barely see in.

"Hold on."

He goes to inspect the area, but Willow prances and grimaces.

"P-please, Dr. P ... I have to pee real bad."

Alder concedes. Any longer delay, and those too-big jeans will be a sagging wet mess. It's freezing as is.

"OK. Fine. Right over there. Please ... be careful. I'm here."

"OK ... Don't go. Please?" she pleads, her eyes meeting his.

From the small distance, her eyes look like two floating emerald gemstones, fixated directly at Alder.

"I won't leave, and I won't let anything hurt you," he whispers. "I promise." He means this from the depths of his being.

Willow steps through the trees and behind the wall of conifers. Gone from Alder's sight. He can still hear the snow pack under her little steps.

Kssh-kssh-kssh.

Alder waits, making this concession out of respect for the privacy that the seven-year-old Willow deserves.

Kssh-kssh.

The sound of her steps disappears.

* * *

It feels like Willow has been gone for an hour—it's been a minute.

"Willow?" Alder's voice cuts sharper than he intends. A chill skates up his spine. "Shit," he hushes under his breath. "Willow?"

"I'm here, Dr. P." She sounds unbothered, but farther away now—too far.

Alder exhales through pursed lips, steadying himself.

"Please … hurry up!"

Kssh … click.

That was closer than Willow's last steps.

The wind shifts suddenly, stirring the pines. They appear to tickle the green-painted sky with their top needles.

Alder inhales, his breath shuttering like a camera burst.

The crunching of Willow's steps resumes. They still sound farther away than expected. The chill from Alder's spine snakes around his ribs and into his armpits.

He stops in his tracks, trying to process the situation. He can barely move his head. He holds his breath, trying not to lose the sound of Willow's little steps.

They return as a nauseating measure of the growing distance between them.

Kssh … kssh … kssh.

Then silence.

Alder hisses, "Willow!"

No reply. She must've lost her sense of direction. *She's only seven. What was I thinking? She was only supposed to go over there. Dumb shit, Aldi!*

Alder walks in Willow's direction and spies a set of large, elongated tracks in the distance. As if something massive lumbered through, dragging handfuls of snakes beside it in the snow.

Then he hears it. That sound from last night. That howling roar of twisting metal, as if something inhuman were being shredded from the inside.

That wasn't the wind, or an animal. That was something *wrong.*

It took out Sheriff Tom, and now it lurks in the night. Perhaps it's right behind him, ready to tear between his shoulder blades, ripping through his torso before his brain can even process the horror.

Alder's heart thumps in his chest, like someone pounding on a window trying to get in. It's so loud he can hear it through his heavy coat. A frantic, rhythmic pulse swells against his eardrums.

Then that familiar and awful smell.

It floods his senses: sickly sweet and metallic, burning at the edges. Then it turns—rancid, gangrenous. Like something pried open and left to fester. The odor fills the back of Alder's throat, which twitches until a gag overtakes him. Saliva fills his mouth, and he repeatedly swallows it back.

"Wi—Willow." His whisper is a rasp, barely more than breath.

She doesn't answer.

That sound. The slithering sound, like a bundle of agitated vipers, draws closer. A slow, rhythmic thumping punctuates it.

The acrid, rotting stench intensifies. The foulest, rankest imaginable, getting worse.

Then Alder realizes those sounds are footsteps. Two sets. Or one set belonging to something moving on all fours.

The crunches quicken. A rhythm emerges. Deeper thumps—faster now. It breaks into a gallop.

Alder's pulse hammers. He whips his head around, searching for Willow. She's not in his line of sight.

He slowly and deliberately steps backward, toward where she should be.

"Willow?"

No answer.

Another step back. His head swivels.

Crack.

His back slams into a pine. The dead basal branches scratch at his neck.

"Shit!" His lips barely form the word before his body locks up.

Alder edges around the tree, closer to where he last saw Willow.

Boomp-boomp-boomp.

Alder peeks into the clearing, tunes out his heart to listen for her.

Willow isn't there. Terror takes on a new flavor. His mind is in a state of panic, under forced restraint—the worst kind.

"Willow?"

Silence is parted by the quickening steps of heavy footfalls approaching.

"DR. P!" Willow screams out.

Alder scrambles toward the sound. He slips once onto a knee but recovers as quickly as he stumbles.

His adrenaline spikes. His heart races, but only to flood blood to his limbs. He hasn't run this fast since fleeing casino "security" in Vegas years ago. He was running for his life then, now he's running for hers.

"WILLOW!" Alder belts out.

"DR. P?" Willow cries out. "P-please, GO AWAY! GOOOO!" Her cries sound thick with tears.

Alder sees Willow sitting with her back against a pine, her face awash with fear, the kind of fear that paralyzes a person. He has not seen this from her until now.

Towering over her is the thing that killed Sheriff Tom. At least seven feet tall, its hulking frame slithers with mucus-covered, snakelike appendages. The vile, writhing things appear to be jutting out from the creature, reaching toward Willow Rose.

The monster's limbs end in razor-sharp, four-fingered claws, which gleam under Goodwin's tail like polished obsidian. The comet's tail reflects in them—more terrifying than beautiful. They make a sickening, metallic slide as it shifts its stance, like knives scraping together.

Alder swallows. His breath hammers. His pulse jackhammers.

He can already see it.

Those claws. Plunging into his chest. Severing his neck, his arteries. Plucking his eyes from their sockets, blinding him before the terminal horror begins. Leaving him in darkness for the rest of the mauling.

Worse, he wouldn't be able to see if Willow got away during all of that. Losing his life, unsure if she would lose her own soon after.

It's that latter thought—the thought of it harming Willow after taking him out—that pulls him back. That can't happen. That won't happen.

Alder's blood rises to a boil as he charges directly toward Willow and the beast.

Whatever strength a human has, he'll use it. At least to give her a chance. *I'm going for the jaw*, he thinks, *no, the neck—dammit, I'll gouge its goddamn eyes out!*

"WILLOW!" Alder screams desperately, shaking his balled fist. "WIL—HEY—GET THE FUCK ON—HEYYYYY—GET AWAY– YOU MUTHA—IMMA FUCK YOU UP—AAAH!"

Alder learned this behavior on the Southside of Chicago. Often, but not always, it's enough to get a threat to retreat. He also knows from experience it works better on the mountain lions in the drunken dark deserts outside of Vegas.

The creature's torso twists away from Willow and toward Alder as he closes in.

"AAAHHHH … HERE I AM, MUFUCKA!"

Alder's war cry mutes, stopping just feet before it. The thing towers over him, scraping the sky.

The monster stares unaffected in Alder's direction. It's difficult to discern if it has pupils. Its burning blue eyes are either looking him in the eyes, at him broadly, or not at all. He can't tell. This alone is unnerving.

"RUN, WILLOW! DAMMIT—Agggh—GO!"

That's Alder's first instinct. Run. But only after Willow is safe. Until then, he's the distraction.

His breath trembles, his chest rises and falls in constricted, uneven waves. The tightness in his stomach makes even shallow breaths difficult.

If those claws tear through his gut, his last meal, Mama Curlie's pancakes, will spill onto the grass along with the rest of his insides.

Alder gives Willow a pleading look. "Willow. Run, please, Willow! Go!"

Willow's green eyes widen briefly, then worry shrinks and moistens them—a reluctant compliance. She crawls to her feet, pauses, and meets Alder's gaze. A tear streaks down her cheek.

"It's OK, Willow. It's going to be OK."

Alder stands between her and the thing, the grotesque form blocking several feet of the space between them.

The little girl wipes her face and sprints for the woods, then stops at the tree line.

"I have to stay. No ... no!"

Willow takes a step back toward them.

"GO, DAMMIT, GOOOOO!" Alder belts out.

Willow flinches. She wipes her face again, then turns and runs, disappearing into the trees.

The monster's eyes stay trained on Alder.

Alder takes a single step back.

The creature watches him, unmoving. Its head tilts as if curious. It doesn't instantly pounce at Alder like it did with Sheriff Tom. Why not? It could have taken both of them down in the blink of an eye, yet it didn't. Alder gets the feeling that the monster is toying with him. It's not a delusion. It appears to watch him more intently than others, and it also seemed to watch Alder while killing Tom. It attacks others but only watches Alder.

Alder takes another step back. Then another.

One step. Two steps ... five steps. Step after step.

Alder silently prays. He tries to telepathically command the beast. *Please stay there!*

If Alder can get some distance, he can run. It's worth a try. *Dammit, this thing is huge.*

Alder's head snaps toward the woods, searching for Willow's blonde hair and green eyes in a field of shimmering snow and trees.

Nothing. Hopefully, she's well beyond sight.

Alder snaps his head back, and his stomach sinks.

It's closer. Without a sound, it's planted itself right in his space.

He stands toe-to-toe with the malicious malefactor.

The nauseating stink assaults his nose and the front of his brain. It's rotten, metallic, damp.

Alder's throat tightens. His own saliva gags him.

The thing doesn't appear to breathe, yet its body shifts, undulating.

The eel-like appendages slither in and out of its flesh, slick and sinuous, making a sloppy, sloshing sound. Tangled snakes, fighting for space—a bowl of worms writhing against each other to reach the center.

What cosmic accident could lead to such a sickening creation?

Alder's gaze locks onto its eyes. Is it smiling?

No, that's just Alder's mind playing tricks. It has no lips, its mouth lined with pointed, razor-sharp teeth. Its face doesn't appear to have the ability for expression. He's anthropomorphizing something that's completely … inhuman.

Alder instinctively averts his gaze down, then reaches for Sheriff Tom's revolver, tucked in the rear of his pants. Then as quick as a whip, he feels his left leg snatched from underneath him—away and upward above his own head. Suddenly, he is looking up at his shoes, with Goodwin's flashing green tail as a backdrop.

Pop.

The revolver goes off, right before he drops it.

For a split second, he feels a sickening sense of weightlessness before the ground rushes toward him.

"NO!" he gasps.

CRAAAACK.

Alder's back slams into the snow-covered dirt—the air is punched out of his lungs.

His scream is cut short by the contact.

He tries to grab at the snow—to push himself through the disorientation and crushing pain ringing through every tissue of his body.

A cold clamp takes his leg again, dragging him.

"FUCK—no! Nooooo ... pl-please stop!"

His fingers scratch the snow, revealing the dirt underneath. Alder claws for something, anything to pull away, secure himself to, or fight back with. There is nothing.

He begs for the monster to release him, but his plea is choked off by the grip around him tightening.

He feels himself go weightless again as his body rises into the night air, like a malfunctioning carnival ride.

The world tilts beneath him as he continues to rise—he feels like he must be at least ten feet in the air now. Sky, trees, and ground all tumble. His stomach lurches, and the blood rushes to his head until—

His body collides with the snow, and his forehead smashes against the cold steel revolver he had just dropped.

Alder lands with such force it leaves a crater in the snow. The violent crash blasts the held breath from his lungs.

Thundering pain erupts across his forehead. His ears ring, and agony drills through his temples.

Alder fights to stay conscious. He lies still as his vision pulses, scintillates at the periphery.

He tries to move, to scramble away, but his body responds at a snail's pace.

The creature still has him, toying with its prey.

Again, a sudden shift of weight. He's effortlessly airborne once more—higher this time. The monster yanks him back down to face level—and holds him there.

It inspects Alder, holding him in its grip like a ragdoll, dangling him by his left leg just inches from its elongated and malformed face. He sways side to side before the abhorrent figure.

Its eyes are fixed. They don't dart. Alder finds it dizzying to try and lock onto them, so he catches the blue flaming peepers as he passes with each swing.

Its eyes are soulless.

They don't hold a message.

They don't communicate wants or demands.

Just concentrated nothingness.

The world ceases to have direction, and vertigo tugs under Alder's jaws, causing him to retch.

He stretches his neck so his face points to the ground, and vomit spews to the snow while he hangs upside down by the left shin. This leg has since gone numb, but the rest of his body is gripped in agony.

Alder gasps for air, but the breath is cut short—another effortless whip to the earth as the creature slams Alder to the ground.

Alder's back arches just as his body collides with the hard, snowy ground. His forehead hits in the same spot as the first forceful crash, causing stars to burst behind his eyelids. The snow melts at his lips, leaving bitter and salty granules of soil on his tongue.

His vision flickers. His mind teeters on the edge of wakefulness. Pressure builds at the back of Alder's neck, surrounding it like a yoke.

A tunnel approaches, then all goes black.

* * *

Alder hears his mother's voice—sharp, her Bajan Creole biting with chastisement.

"The good Lord don't condone no rasshole vices, and neither do I— not in my house! Where did you get those? Where, Aldi?"

Alder stutters. He wants to say his uncle Shem, and he'd be telling the truth. But he doesn't. He doesn't want to play the snitch role right now. Besides, Uncle Shem is cool.

Alder remembers standing in the tiny kitchen of their Southside apartment on 83rd and South Paulina Street, his mother's eyes fierce as he grips a deck of playing cards in his twelve-year-old fist. A medical encyclopedia is sprawled open beneath them.

Nina Graham was gentle, always—until it came to gambling, or anything else that defied "the Lord's word."

Nina worked as a cleaning lady in a clinic and would sneak books about medicine home for Alder to read. From a young age, he was fascinated with the human body and how to fix a broken one. Of course, she couldn't afford these texts on her pay as a single adoptive mother, but she always got him what he needed—and found a way to get him the things he wanted. She was loving, but she didn't spare the rod in the least.

She caught him, and he got the worst whoopin' of his life.

Until—

"Shhhh." Alder sucks through his teeth.

He regains consciousness. To that grating, inhuman screech.

The noise cuts.

Resumes.

Alder thinks he's being swallowed whole.

No.

The creature is on its back, convulsing, its limbs thrashing as if something unseen has seized control of its body.

Pain flares up the right side of Alder's face. His breath is uneven, shallow. He's on the verge of fainting—again.

A small hand grips his arm. Shaking him.

"Dr. P! Please!"

It's Willow.

Alder blinks rapidly. He clenches his lids, trying to focus his vision. His mind is in dizzying disarray.

He sits up in time to see the creature flailing on the ground. Snow mixed with dirt and pebbles sprays against Willow and Alder.

The thing tries to stand but reels back to the ground. It scratches wildly, claws carving deep into the snow, exposing the soil underneath. It tries to rise again, coiling.

It can't.

Then, it stops suddenly. Its mouth twists into an ember-lit grin. It turns toward them—watching. Still. Too still.

It sizes them up. The writhing appendages on its body go still then rise, pointing outward, seeking Alder and Willow. All the while, the creature holds its unblinking stare.

They both push to their feet, her small hands gripping his arm, trembling. His head pounds. Warm blood oozes down his right cheek. His vision blurs again, the world tilts. His balance wavers, both legs are unsteady beneath him, but he feels a slight surge of adrenaline ... no, something else—a pulse that isn't his own.

Ahead, the creature lingers, a massive, unnatural blur at the edges of his failing vision.

Alder's vision clears in time to see the snakes—no, not snakes, something else ... resume their opposing slither in and out of the monster's core, which appears painful. He can't identify them.

It keeps its eyes locked on them. Then it rolls, twisting unnaturally.

Its midsection turns first, like a threaded pipe, lower limbs locking into the earth. Then its upper half unwinds, rising to all fours.

It jerks backward—wrong, off-kilter—then rears onto its hind legs, broad antlers pointing high into the air.

It lets out its skull-clattering screech again, making Alder grimace against his slicing headache.

The creature convulses—sharply, violently. The wet crack of shifting bones and snapping tendons splits the air. Its body seizes, contorts ... like something fighting itself from the inside out.

Then, it collapses to all fours and bolts away.

It tears through the pines with the brute force of a grizzly, the speed of a jaguar.

The shriek echoes in Alder's cranium as he attempts to focus both his vision and his brain, his sensorium a swirling mass of blurred shapes and muffled noise.

What do we do now?

All goes black.

CHAPTER SIX

"Dr. P, please wake up."

Alder stirs, pulled from the deep, dragging dark by the sound of her voice. Small. Frantic. On the edge of breaking.

Cold nips at his face. Wind creeps under his coat, riding up his ribs. Snow melts on his skin. His jaw aches underneath his numb cheek.

His lips are numb, but he tastes grit—a mouthful of snow and blood.

He groans, shifts. Something warm presses against his left side.

Willow.

She's there. She stayed.

"Dr. P … you wouldn't wake up. We have to go."

A monster is out here, hunting them, and she stayed with him.

Alder blinks through the haze, and a sensation settles over him. Something he can't see—something beyond the clearing. A presence.

The thought of it clinging to the trees, peeking around them, buried in the darkness. Watching. Waiting.

It's there.

Somewhere in the black—suspended, maybe hanging. Perched on the trunk like an animal—or something pretending to be one.

The weight of it is unbearable—like a lead blanket on his chest.

He sways but forces himself upright. His legs wobble beneath him, rubbery and weak. His vision winks in and out.

The nausea fades. Not gone, just … lurking.

Willow grabs his hand and pulls.

"We have to go, Dr. P. We have to go!"

She tries to hold him up, bracing under his arm, but she's too small. Her effort is a child's determination against something insurmountable.

He stumbles forward.

Alder spots the dropped revolver and quickly snatches it, tucking it into his pants.

It starts again.

The nausea. The spinning. The weight in his skull.

His knees buckle, and he stops, retching. Dry-heaving. Nothing comes up. Just pain, peeling his brain apart from the inside.

Through the blur: a cottage.

Warm porch lights glowing like a painful beacon, wreathed in a halo of torture.

Alder stares. His vision waves at the edges.

A chance.

A car, maybe.

A way out.

Morningstar Falls Medical Center is still a few miles away.

Walking isn't an option. Not like this. There's hope.

They move fast. Or at least, they try to.

Each step sends cymbal-crashing pain into Alder's dome.

Goodwin's tail flares above, burning across the sky. The streaking glow splinters Alder's vision into ribbons of nausea.

He tightens his grip on Willow's hand, half-dragging, half-guiding her forward.

*　*　*

The cottage is secluded. Isolated. Maybe half a mile from where they started.

As they near, the air shifts. Carried on the wind comes a scent: warm, rich, unmistakably cooking.

Willow's stomach growls under the sound of the breeze.

At least it's not the monster.

Poor thing hasn't eaten all day—and hasn't once complained.

Alder and Willow arrive at the empty wraparound porch. She tries to steady him as they reach the steps.

Halfway up, something catches Alder's eye.

Inside, two men talk in a dimly lit kitchen—the only lit room in the cottage. A long tapestry drapes the door—an intricate quilt stitched with a bold, starlike pattern. To the right, an unpainted wooden carving stands. Two trees. Their roots stretch beneath a glass panel—tangled under the surface. They reach for each other. Intertwining. Bound.

Something tugs at Alder's mind. A flicker of memory. Familiar. His eyes widen.

He searches his thoughts, but his concussed brain refuses to give.

Alder lifts a hand and knocks softly.

A sound to the right. Breathy, unnatural.

Clicking. Chittering.

Like a giggle—but not quite.

Alder starts, instinct pulling him back. He yanks Willow behind him, turning toward the sound.

The woods hold their breath.

Then, movement at the door.

Through the upper window, covered only by a sheer curtain, a shadow shifts.

A ripple of fabric.

Then, the curtain pulls aside.

A man peers through. His eyes land on Alder, then Willow.

The curtain falls back into place.

Silence.

The door opens with a creak.

A man in his thirties stands on the threshold. Short, neat haircut.

An Ojibwe medallion rests at the base of his neck—its beads telling stories of a proud culture.

On his wrist, a Casio G-Shock. A quiet contradiction.

"Hello."

His voice is calm.

Then his gaze lands on Alder. On the blood. And his voice drops.

"Welcome?"

Alder tries to speak. Pain clamps his skull in a vice. Even opening his mouth feels like someone is tightening a wrench around his throat.

"Sir! My name is—" His breath catches, the effort too much. He pushes forward. "Alder. This … is Willow."

The man says nothing. Simply listens while wearing a stoic expression. Waiting.

Alder needs a question. A reaction. Something. Anything that leads to help and not a bullet in the chest for trespassing. He realizes just how this looks. He wouldn't trust himself under these circumstances either.

He swallows. "Hey … I'm Alder. We're in trouble. You too! Something—it's out there." His urgency rattles his skull. "Shiiiit!"

The man stands there, brow furrowed.

"I'm sorry, there's something—please," Alder forces out.

Nothing. The man holds his silence, as if waiting for more. Maybe an explanation about what left Alder looking like a "Thriller" music video extra.

Alder forces himself to keep going.

"H-hospital … Morningstar Falls. I'm a doctor—Peony."

At this, the man's expression flickers. His mouth parts slightly.

"Oh yeah." He nods. "I know you! You took care of my father yesterday. I saw your name on his discharge papers—I'm Frank." He reaches out his hand.

Alder blinks hard.

"What?"

"Sepsis ... urine infection," the man continues.

Alder's brow furrows.

"Your dad? Mr. Benoit?" His voice is hoarse, disbelieving. "He's home ... already?"

Frank answers, "He signed out AMA as soon as I got to the hospital from work. He made me drive him home."

He sighs.

"He's a stubborn man ... It's his belief. He'd rather let nature take its course ... plus, he hates needles. He's all like, 'They take blood every morning, Frank!'"

Alder shakes his head, pressing a finger to his temple. "I recall ... something ... ugh."

Frank continues, "He said he had to leave before the darkness swallowed the helpers."

Alder straightens, a chill rippling through his spine.

"Hey ... wh-wha does that mean? Helpers—" His voice edges on desperation. "Darkness swallowing the helpers? Can you—"

Frank cuts him off.

"You can ask him yourself."

He steps aside, holding the door open.

"Here, come in."

As Alder and Willow stumble into the dimly lit foyer, the blood, scuffs, and bruises become more visible. Frank winces.

"Woah ... Doc, what in the hell happened?"

*　　*　　*

Alder and Willow are led into the small cottage in the middle of nowhere. Pines surround the home in all directions, their dark forms pressing in. The cottage must sit about a mile off Gunmetal Road, far enough out that no one would hear a scream.

Willow's concerned green eyes stay locked on Alder. She holds her small hands up as if trying to catch him, should he fall.

They had stumbled all the way here, fueled by fear—by the knowledge that something was out there. Stalking them.

Mr. Benoit sits on a stool at his kitchen counter, slicing an apple with a pocketknife. The blade glints under the dim light as he carves off a neat sliver.

"The trees grow toward the light," he says. "Welcome."

Alder shakes his head, still catching his breath. "This is insane. You were septic, Mr. Benoit. You should be in a hospital bed, not here slicing apples."

His son, Frank, pulls a second stool up to the counter across from Mr. Benoit. Alder sinks onto it, his right elbow landing with a dull thud, his head following into his open palm. He grimaces.

Frank pulls open the freezer and grabs a bag of frozen peas. He hands them to Alder, who presses it against his forehead. The cold hits like a hammer at first, but is followed by mild relief.

He cracks open a squinted eye. Willow's face is a nest of concern—pink, trembling, and on the verge of tears. She stands next to him, refusing the seat Frank placed for her.

Alder saves the energy of rapid blinking, keeping his eyes closed in the brightly lit kitchen. It's eccentrically decorated but clean—lived-in. Definitely the home of two men. A framed photo rests on a curio shelf. Frank's mom, Mrs. Benoit? She was beautiful. Maybe still is, if she's alive.

Mr. Benoit waves the knife lazily, slices another piece of apple, and slides it between his teeth.

Frank exhales. "Yeah, he does that, Doc. The second he's coherent enough to sign himself out and prove he's competent … he's gone."

Mr. Benoit shrugs, chewing. "A gloom is coming. It will swallow the haven of the helpers—swallow the helpers too." He sets down his knife. "I'd rather take my chances here."

Alder straightens, frowning. "What are you saying? Just tell me straight. Is the hospital in danger?"

Frank lifts a hand as if to brush it off, but Alder doesn't let it go. "No. I need to know. These visions." His voice sharpens. "There's something out there. It's real. And it's already killed Sheriff Tom."

The blade stills against the apple's flesh.

Mr. Benoit looks up slowly. "Tom was my friend. A good man." His voice softens. "It didn't feast well on him."

He studies Alder's face, and something in his expression shifts. "He's dead."

A certainty. As if he already knew.

He exhales, long and slow. "The heavens have opened," he murmurs. "He was an irritant intended to be a balm—but the Windigo's sickness runs too deep."

Alder blinks. "Balm? Windigo?"

Mr. Benoit nods. "It suffers. Feels the hunger like fire in its bones. The only way to quiet it? Swallow everything whole. No scraps, no remains."

Alder presses his fingers into his temples. His voice is low. "So it has to kill—to eat—to stop the pain?"

Mr. Benoit leans forward, eyes sharp. "Ah-ha! Yes! The darkness: greed, gluttony, hate. You know 'em all. That's the essence it craves. It knows where to find it too. There's a little bit in everyone, but some people—well, they're overflowing with the bad shit." His glassy eyes dart to Alder, scanning around his body as if watching a fly buzzing about him.

Mr. Benoit continues, "Tom couldn't satiate it. Too good of a man." He exhales, shaking his head. "It will still kill. Always. Without thought, without restraint."

His voice drops lower, almost reverent. "It swallows them all, and in doing so, it feeds. The more darkness it consumes, the more it can calm its pain. That's just it. It's greedy. And it will never find its fill." He chuckles. "Darkness swallows darkness. And there's always more of that, eh?"

Alder's breath catches. He says the name again and it sends a chill through his ribs. "Windigo."

"The Windigo can take many forms, but its hunger is always the same … break apart. Consume."

He pauses while slicing off another piece of apple, then resumes. "All those good people, they lie in torment. It holds their spirit, makes them feel the guilt it feels … hoping their suffering will quench its own pain."

Mr. Benoit slides the apple slice into his mouth, and his eyes appear misty.

In a flash, his demeanor changes from somber to animated. He wipes his thumb on his pant leg and takes only two crunching chews before swallowing the apple slice.

His lips part slightly, as if something final is about to spill from him.

Instead, he chuckles. A strange, stilted sound. Not from humor, but something else. Something broken.

Mr. Benoit suddenly stiffens, his body wracked by a tremor, his fevered eyes becoming glassy. He points at Willow, just as he did at the hospital.

"Your roots must sink deep," he whispers. "Find the other tree. Or fall alone."

Willow and Alder lock eyes.

For a moment, neither of them speaks.

Alder feels it: a pull, a thread twisting between them, something he had ignored before. Not just fear. Not just survival. Something older, something inevitable.

Mr. Benoit chuckles again, a sharp cackle.

Alder looks over at Frank, the only coherent adult in the room. "Is there a way we can get a ride to the hospital? Please."

Frank exhales, rubbing a hand down his face. "Yeah. Sure. I'll drive you." He gestures vaguely at his father. "I need to bring him back anyway, as you can see. We'll see how many days of antibiotics they can pour into him before he runs off again."

"Thank you." Alder presses his hands together.

*   *   *

Alder, Willow, Mr. Benoit, and Frank climb into the pickup truck. Frank takes the wheel and pulls onto the road near the Benoit home.

Alder squints, his head pounding. "Not Gunmetal?"

"Nah, Doc. Shortcut. We'll get there quicker this way." Frank eyes Alder through the rearview mirror.

Alder nods, resting his throbbing head against the cool back window. A goose egg is forming beneath the scrape on his head.

Willow gazes out at the night sky.

Above them, meteors wink in the comet's tail like dying embers, burning as they slip through the atmosphere.

On the back of the passenger seat, a ball-headed war club rests in a worn leather sheath—a two-ended Ojibwe weapon, honed for crushing and piercing.

Mr. Benoit smiles proudly. "I carved it out of a fell piece of wood— from the twin tree." He gestures broadly, in no specific direction, before shaking his head. "I can't remember where that was—that hidden place."

He points to the sky. His hands sway, then lower sharply—his voice deepens. "The lightning provided the wood ... a green flash." He looks at his palms. "My hands did the rest ... I was sick out of my gourd that day."

Mr. Benoit pats his son's shoulder proudly. "Thanks to my ancestors for leading my boy out there to me."

Willow's eyes study the weapon.

She reaches for it. Slowly.

Alder notices. "Nuh-uh. Leave that alone. Dangerous."

From the front seat, Mr. Benoit pulls down the visor mirror, meeting her gaze through the reflection.

"Go on," he says. "Feel it. See for yourself."

Willow hesitates, glancing at Alder.

He shakes his head—not a full no, but something hesitant. Something that leaves space for a yes.

A long beat.

"Go ahead."

With unexpected reverence, Willow slides the weapon out of the sheath.

The wood is smooth and adorned with intricately colored threading.

A two-inch-long, sharp point is on one end. The other end has a solid wooden ball.

A carving runs down the long staff: a feather painted in intricate green and gray. It shimmers, as if imbued with something more.

Even in the dim light, the blade glistens. Faint gold flecks shimmer—like the meteorite that morning.

Flecks that eventually disappeared.

Alder frowns—noticing the sharp end. Something about it feels familiar.

"Wait … hang on." He exhales sharply. "What's going on here?"

In the front seat, Mr. Benoit and Frank exchange a knowing glance.

"A new beginning," says Mr. Benoit.

He and his son chuckle quietly.

Frank finally speaks, "Don't be afraid. It's filled with the breath of our ancestors. Sage grounds it; tobacco opens it for another."

He pauses.

"Like I said, my dad is a seer. What you call magic is what we have always known. Spirit moves through all things—earth, water, fire, sky. This is how we listen. This is how we see. And this is how we remember."

Willow turns the weapon in her hands, studying it with quiet curiosity. Her brow furrows.

The shimmer deepens.

Alder hears it—thinks he hears it—a low-frequency hum just

beneath perception.

The weapon glows, a flickering, unsustained gold in her hands.

Alder watches, his stomach knotting as Willow turns the club carelessly. Barely able to hold it in her tiny hands, she tries to adjust her finger positions, figuring out how to handle it. The sharp edge on the bottom end glints in the dim light of the rear-seat console.

Alder slowly holds out a hand.

"Gimme dat—please."

Willow passes it to him.

The moment Alder's fingers curl around the handle, a warm tingle rushes up his right arm. It spreads, pouring into his armpit and surging toward his chest.

For a moment, he feels light. Whole. At peace. His breath catches. He exhales sharply, looking up.

Through the visor mirror, Mr. Benoit is watching him.

Grinning.

"You like that, huh?" His voice is steady, knowing. "Gave it a warrior's name. One with legacy."

Alder hesitates. "Yeah? What's that?"

Mr. Benoit grins. "Sarah." He chuckles, a throaty *hup-hup-hup.*

From the driver's seat, Frank shakes his head and snickers. He glances up in the rearview. "Dad's a sci-fi guy. Sarah Connor, right?"

Mr. Benoit's throaty cackle fills the car again.

Alder isn't sure what to take seriously. Even from the backseat, he can feel the fever radiating off the old man's body.

The laughter fades. Mr. Benoit's voice lowers, turning slow and certain.

"Take it! Let it protect you—protect the others." He pauses, closing his eyes. "*Niizh mitigoon gaye wiinawaa giiwitaawag miinawaa gii-giizhiitaawag* Windigo."

Mr. Benoit's eyes flutter open. His gaze, clouded with delirium, fixes on Alder.

"Two trees stand together. What is lost will return."

Alder lifts an eyebrow but doesn't argue. He accepts the gift.

"Thank you."

This is all crazy. The Windigo. The visions. The comet. All of it.

But it feels right.

Laying Sarah in his lap, Alder leans his head back against the window. The cold is a partial relief. His eyelids grow heavy.

Frank glances at Alder in the rearview. "Where ya from, Doc? If you don't mind me asking."

"Chicago … Southside."

"Ah! So, you like Kanye West?"

Alder cracks open one eye.

"He's a'ight."

Frank presses a button on the stereo—of course, he's got a Kanye West CD queued.

"Through the Wire" plays.

Mr. Benoit starts bobbing his head.

Alder turns to Willow. Through his single squinted eye, he sees her bouncing in her seat, pumping a tiny fist high to the beat.

Alder shakes his head slightly and closes his eyes.

Frank looks through the mirror, turning down the volume. "Doc, I'm sorry, boss."

Alder replies while still looking at Willow. Though each tinny hi-hat beat pierces his eardrums, he can't take it away from her. Kids possess superhero coping abilities amidst trauma.

"It's all good … just a little lower, though … please."

"You got it, Doc."

*   *   *

The pickup truck roves down an old, barely paved road, dipping in and out of the pines, its tires crackling against patches of frost. The creek below is frozen over, the wooden planks of the manmade bridge groaning under the truck's weight as they pass.

Alder's eyes flicker open.

The faint glow of Curlie's Diner pulses in the distance, like a dying ember—weak and wrong. A shadow creeps into his gut, the cold grip of unease.

"Hey, Frank, can we stop over at the diner? Check on Mama Curlie?"

Frank exhales. "Of course."

They pull off the trail onto the narrow-paved road leading up to the diner. The place is unusually dark.

Alder flips open his phone. Nine p.m. No messages. No signal.

He watches the battery icon blink empty just before the screen dies.

"Dammit," he whispers.

She doesn't close for another hour. It shouldn't be this dark. Only a faint, dim light struggles through the windows.

As they pull in front of the diner, Alder sees it.

Blood.

Spattered across the snow, over the steps leading inside.

Frank tenses, hands gripping the wheel. "What the hell?"

Alder's heart pounds. The sensation is immediate: dread crawling up his spine, settling in his ribs like a tightening vice.

"No. No. No, no, no, no, no, no—"

He yanks off his seatbelt, wrestles with the door latch, and leaps out into the cold. He falls onto a knee but recovers.

The backup generator hums from the rear of the diner. No movement in the windows.

Alder stares at the blood. A ten-foot-long spray leading up to the stairs. The edges of the splatter are already pink with frost, darkening along the thickest parts. Someone was retreating for their dear life. Their last breaths used to claw the snow in a futile attempt to escape.

"Mama Curlie," Alder mutters under his breath.

She's the only one who calls him Aldi. He's the only one who calls her Mama Curlie.

His legs nearly give out, but he fights to keep his footing, fueled by fear of what he already knows.

"KID! COME B—" Frank starts, but his voice is cut short.

A car door slams.

Crunch.

Tiny, quick footsteps in the snow.

Alder is frozen in shock.

Willow stands beside him, small and unyielding.

"Get … back … in … the car." His voice is quiet but firm.

She doesn't move.

Alder turns his head slowly and looks at her, his jaw clenched.

"I said, get back in the car."

She shakes her head.

"Not again!" Willow says, defiance flickering in her eyes.

Alder's throat tightens. "Dammit, Willow." His voice breaks. Tears blur his vision. "Willow. Get back in the car! NOW!"

Willow doesn't flinch. Instead, she takes his hand. Her small, warm fingers tremble in his cold palm.

She squeezes. Harder, now with both hands.

"We have to stay together. Always."

Alder sucks in a breath through his teeth. His throat burns. He scoops her up without a word; his unsteady legs feel a little lighter. He walks her back to the truck and sets her inside. After this, he nearly falls again—his balance is shot.

"You got child locks?" His voice is tight.

Frank nods.

Alder exhales. "Turn. Them. On," he says as he closes the door, averting his eyes from Willow.

Click.

Alder turns back toward the diner, his boots crunching in the bloody snow.

He stops at the base of the stairs, hesitating.

The driver's door groans as Frank opens it. "Doc, be careful!" he yells. "What the fu—"

Willow vaults over the center console and dives out through the open driver's door. She nearly stumbles as she lands clumsily on her tiny feet.

Alder barely has time to react. She runs, frantically, straight to him.

"No!" His voice catches in his throat.

She doesn't stop. She slams into his side, pressing close. Desperate.

"We have to stay together—always."

Alder exhales sharply, gripping her hand. He's not winning this.

"Stay right next to me." His voice is raw. "If something happens, run back to the truck."

Willow nods as she maintains a tight grip.

They step inside the diner.

* * *

The diner appears empty.

Flickering backup lights carve jagged shadows across the booths, sinking into the green vinyl seats.

The jukebox hums at the back, glowing a sickly green. "Shark Attack" by the Wailing Souls stutters through the speakers—looping the same initial seven seconds of the song, over and over again in a seamless skip.

Alder sways. A thick, citrusy, peppery rot floods his chest, his stomach twisting.

Willow buries her face against his arm.

His eyes lock onto a bloodied babushka scarf near the counter.

His breath stutters—inhaling suddenly takes effort.

A slow drip echoes from the kitchen.

He moves forward, past the counter, stepping into the kitchen.

He turns.

Syrupy, dark blood trickles from the range hood, cutting through the glow of the jukebox spilling in from the diner's pass-through cutout.

If this thing feeds on the humors of evil, it must have consumed Mama Curlie with deep frustration. Because she had none.

Suddenly, there's banging from outside the diner.

Frank's horn blares, then cuts silent.

A loud, blood curdling war cry rings. "YEEEAAAAAAAAH." Silence slices it short.

Alder yanks Willow's hand and bolts for the front, bursting out of the diner.

As the door flies open, he sees Mr. Benoit holding the club. He lets out a war cry. He rears back with the little strength his septic body has, but the monster latches onto the front of Mr. Benoit's neck mid-scream, cutting it off with a guttural snap, like a number two pencil breaking.

The worm-like appendages writhe and jitter like a rattlesnake's tail. Blood sprays in all directions, and the slithering worms appear to chase after the squirting streams.

The monster lumbers up onto its back legs, then turns to the steps, where Willow and Alder stand frozen in place. A second splash of bloody snow lies at its feet, which means it must've made short work of Frank.

Alder chokes back vomit. Watching this ... again a witness to another life snatched up by this thing ... it rips at something primal inside himself.

A vision flashes, brief but blinding.

It's of everyone he knows—suffering the same fate.

If they haven't already.

Alder feels it: heat rising up his arms, stoking a fire deep in his gut.

Now, quiet. Motionless. Between the truck and diner, a towering monstrosity. Even from five steps below the porch, it looms at eye level—too still, too present—waiting.

Its broad spray of antlers stretches into a jagged, unnatural silhouette, warped by the sickly glow of Goodwin's tail.

Fear stills Alder's breath.

Mr. Benoit's fevered blood drips from its face, steaming in the cold.

The blood fades as the creature absorbs it. Crimson to pink as it seeps in—leaving behind the ashen gray of its wormy flesh.

A sickly orange glow escapes through the gaps between its knifelike teeth, illuminating the hollow spaces of its incompletely sealed mouth.

The creature's eyes burn like blue lanterns hanging at the mouths of two narrow, shadowed corridors with arched ceilings—deep, hollow, and endless.

They snap toward Willow.

Alder yanks her coat, pulling her behind him.

His left hand creeps behind his back, fingers curling around Sheriff Tom's revolver. This hand is clumsy. He fumbles—nearly drops it—but catches the grip before it falls.

He cocks the hammer.

Aims.

The Windigo's eyes flick to the weapon. Then back to Alder.

Alder pulls the trigger.

Pop.

The creature doesn't move.

The bullet shears off the tip of an antler—a spark flickers.

Pop.

Pop.

Pop.

Click.

Each shot hit the creature's snaking flesh with a thick and heavy thud.

The gun is empty. Sheriff Tom used one bullet, Alder wasted one in his forest fight.

A wave of nausea hits Alder. He can feel himself entering a tunnel of darkness, one that leads to him hitting the ground.

"Ssshit!" he says with tight jaws, afraid to move a muscle.

The Windigo stands there, still and silent. How can this abominable thing be stopped? So far, the only thing that seems to have any effect is being near Willow. The only thing that gives it pause, at least.

Alder holds Willow behind him with one arm. With his other hand, he grips the empty revolver. He's afraid to drop it—or to make any movements for that matter.

"Run—inside! Now, Willow! Go all the way in. Hide somewhere really good!"

As he nudges Willow behind him, he feels resistance and her small hands tugging back at him.

"Now! Go!" He pushes at her. "Go—"

"No. No, we gotta stay together," Willow says with defiance.

She pulls at whatever material of Alder's coat and clothes she can as he tries to urge her along.

"Please, Willow! Get in there now."

Alder can feel her swatting away his hands and pulling herself closer by grabbing his coattail. He keeps his eyes trained on the monster, which, for some reason, has not attacked.

"Dammit, Willow."

Willow pulls herself tightly against Alder's waist. "We stay together."

Then, with sudden and jarring force, the Windigo drops onto all fours, its stance uneven, tilted upward as if its body were never meant to move this way—its front limbs longer than the rear.

It screams.

The sound lances through Alder's skull as it revs down.

Willow clutches his hand with a firmness disproportionate to her small size.

The Windigo shifts again. Then, with a grotesque, snapping motion, its head whips toward the trees. It darts into the woods, west—straight toward Morningstar Falls Medical Center.

The pines and brush thrash violently as the massive creature crashes through them, their tops swaying against the ember-streaked sky, silhouetted against Goodwin's green, sparkling tail.

A second, splitting scream rips through the night.

It cuts to silence.

The first seven seconds of "Shark Attack" continue to loop faintly from inside the diner.

"Faith," Alder mutters.

He snatches Willow up into his arms and bolts for the truck.

As gently as possible, he tosses her into the passenger seat.

"Seatbelt!"

Willow complies, her little hand reaching back in haste.

Alder scrambles to the driver's side, stumbling once.

His blurred vision locks onto the war club, half-buried in the snow.

Blood smears the handle. The men tried to use it. In vain.

Something compels Alder to take it, and he doesn't hesitate. Instinct moves him to yank it from the snow.

A jolt arcs up his arm, locking his grip around the club. He couldn't drop it if he tried.

It's like grabbing a live wire—startling, but not painful—held in place by an unseen hand atop his, unlike anything he's ever felt before.

His headache pulses, but beneath it, something steadies him. He feels stronger.

Alder jumps into the driver's seat. Inside the truck, away from immediate danger, the club's current fades—just slightly.

The energy softens, no longer pulsing against his palm.

He lays Sarah gently on the console between himself and Willow. The war club glows, brighter now. A steady shimmer of vibrant, sparkling motes floats outward, hangs midair, then drifts slowly toward the club.

Alder shoves the key ignition. The engine roars to life, the tires bite into the snow, and he peels off onto Gunmetal Road.

Toward the hospital. Toward the Windigo.

He flips open his Razr. No signal. But he dials anyway.

Boop. Nothing.

"Faith!" He takes a deep breath, then exhales a sharp breath. "Arrrrggh—move, truck … Move, dammit!"

Alder cares for Faith, and he's suppressed it this whole time. He cannot imagine bringing the weight of his karma onto her. Or the thought of that thing doing to her what it did to Tom.

The Kanye West CD blasts through the speakers. "Through the Wire."

He fumbles at the buttons, accidentally skipping backward several times to another song.

Alder's vision blurs. His skull feels like it's caving in. He grips the wheel, fighting to keep steady beneath Goodwin's tail, flaring across the sky, its embers drifting like dying stars, dimly lighting the way.

"All Falls Down" by Kanye West pounds through the truck stereo. The tinny sound from the factory speakers rattles his head.

Between the dumb layout of the buttons, his blurred vision, and his rising panic, he can't turn it off.

Or down.

Willow isn't bouncing. She isn't dancing.

Through the haze, he sees her—a small silhouette in a red puffer coat, rigid in the seat, except her head—which snaps side to side, searching.

The trees zip past outside of the vehicle, moonlit openings between them stutter like a flip-book.

Alder slaps his hand clumsily at the stereo controls. "All Falls Down" cuts to Bart Ellis's "Behold a Dark Horse."

"So—yeah, that's it … like time-lagged echoes of the s—[static]. A fr—[static]—wormho—rrrriii—ght!"

Willow reaches over and turns the dial until it clicks off.

She turns to Alder, who can only make out a blurred, fair circle: her face, dotted by her green eyes.

"Dr. P—I remember … a little … I'm not from here."

Alder's spine stiffens. "What do y—?"

"It's like here, but somewhere else … everything was different. Donkey Kong was Jumpman. The ketchup at Mama Curlie's, it had a different name too."

She wipes a tear and continues. "I was stuck in a tiny room, and I couldn't turn around. It was dark behind me … so I kept walking until I got here. I don't remember anymore … I'm sorry."

The blurred image of Willow wiping her eyes with her forearm makes Alder queasy. He knows that she has been strong, too strong, up until now. He feels the weight pressing onto her shaky ground, her sense of security slipping. He's experienced similar in the past. The searching of adult faces for strength. For someone that has it all under control. It's a grim feeling when the search comes up empty. When you look to those to keep you safe, only to find the same insecurity and fear in their expressions.

Not only that, but her cryptic recollections add to the jagged dread of the moment. She's clearly lost more than he ever has. Not just her mother, if Clara was her mother, but also her memories. An existential crisis at seven years of age—a dreadful thought.

Alder tries his best to make sense of it. He's an educated man, a man of science. Because of this, he carries a healthy amount of skepticism in his back pocket. But this … this is like a ton of bricks, and it pulverizes the devil's advocate in him. His skepticism can't protect his fragile existence at the moment. This actually makes sense, even if he doesn't understand fully. It's the only thing that makes friggin' sense.

No doubt some of those memories are happy, and now they are

gone. All she seems to have are the moments here, with Alder.

"It's OK. We're going to figure this out ... OK?"

Just speaking causes pain to ripple through Alder's head.

"I can't go back—it's all gone. I want to stay, with you."

Alder opens his mouth to respond. He pauses, not only because of the pain rattling his dome, but also because of the surreality of the moment. Though he can't confirm or deny either way, this all may be a state of delirium—a product of a traumatic brain injury of huge proportions.

CHAPTER SEVEN

The ER is mostly empty at MSFMC, just Faith and Russ at the nurse's station.

Faith's eyes are trained on a novel—but her mind is on Willow and Alder. She's been meaning to call but doesn't want to hover.

A few feet away, Russ's thumbs pitter-patter on her Game Boy.

A hospital cordless rings on the counter in front of Faith. She folds a corner of her page and sets the book down.

Beep.

"Hello?" Static. "Hello?"

Nothing.

Her stomach knots. Something doesn't feel right. Even amidst the other weirdness, this is different.

Dread unfolding in a familiar shape.

The same dread she used to get when he came home from work.

Most nights were OK. But if he got a few cans of Colson down, she knew what was coming.

She used to count them—calculating when she could sneak out, or at least hide away until he passed out.

She didn't run for a long time, thinking: *He's a good man deep down.*

Just help him through another day, and he'll be the man I married again ... but that day wouldn't come. She wouldn't run until he nearly killed her.

Miss Curlie took Faith in. She was more than a shelter—she was a mother to most around here. An angel.

And yet, despite the safety—the healing—Faith still wears a heavy blanket of loneliness in Morningstar Falls.

Until ... Dr. Alder Peony arrived.

She felt it from the moment he shook her hand. That tug. Magic.

He's not interested. At least that's what she tells herself. He's avoidant—but every time she draws near, he stiffens, blushes.

Hope, maybe?

She's thought about it. If he stayed. If she left with him. Silly thoughts, really.

They haven't even gone on a date—but she's imagined the life.

One where raised hands mean affection, not fear. Where he touches her cheek only to soothe.

Faith stares into space, lost in her fantasy, until a stench wafts into the nurse's station.

Russ scrunches her face. "Oh ... my god ... what is that?"

She pauses her Game Boy and jumps up, heading toward triage where the smell seems to be strongest.

"Ugh. Must be the sewer," Faith says.

"No way. That's not sewage. That smells wrong," Russ calls back.

Faith checks her watch. "Where's Jennings? He's been gone two hours."

Russ chuckles. "Girl, you know where he is."

They glance at each other. Faith tries to fight the smirk curling at her lip, but they both crack up.

Then, from the west, a faint shrieking sound.

Faith and Russ hush.

From the east: tires screeching. A growling engine in the lot.

* * *

The pickup groans as Alder speeds across the hospital's empty lot, a scowl carved deep into his face.

Above, Goodwin's tail flickers with rising intensity, casting eerie, shifting shadows from the surrounding pines onto the pavement.

The overhead lights pulse too, making the shadows vanish, then reappear.

The glass doors of the entrance are dim, the flashing reflections blinding the view inside. It looks abandoned.

Alder screeches to a stop in front of the entrance—illegally. Who cares? There's a soul-eating monster stalking through Morningstar Falls. They can put a sticker on the window. And another on the Windigo's lumpy forehead.

"Stay there. I'm coming around," he says to Willow.

She nods and stays put.

Alder grabs the war club and scrambles out, stumbling as his leg hitches once, then catches.

He rounds the truck and clumsily grabs the passenger door. It takes two tries with his left hand, but he gets it open and lifts Willow out.

As he sets her down, he grips her tiny hand, and a surge rips up his right arm.

His vision sharpens. The hitch in his leg vanishes.

He looks down at Willow, confused at first, but something is starting to click. *What she said. It all makes sense.*

"But … how?" he whispers.

They rush to the entrance.

The doors don't open.

Alder releases Willow's hand and tries to pry them apart. His sight blurs again.

He presses his face to the glass, scanning for movement.

To the left, through the triage area, something shifts.

Alder hammers at the glass with the edge of his fist.

It's Russ.

He sees her silhouette—the ponytail, the quick spin of her head.

She holds up a finger and hurries to the door. She flicks a switch above, and the doors slide apart—a rush of air flutters Russ's loose bangs.

Before Alder can say anything, Willow bolts forward, slamming into

Russ, her arms locking tight around her waist.

She staggers back with a sharp exhale. "Oof. Hey, pun'kin. Where ya been?"

Alder shoots her a look of concern. "Where is everyone?"

"Just me, Faith, and Doc Jennings," Russ replies. "No patients all day. Jennings went to the cafeteria hours ago—hasn't come back. Probably off with Claudia from med-surg. Gross, right?"

Russ blurs at the edges.

Alder tries to blink it clear, but his vision only gets worse.

His headache cranks up—like someone is bending the pole meant to hold up his scalp.

Alder steps into the dim light. He lifts a brow. "Why are you still here?"

Russ's face shifts, concerned now. "Vin went home. Roland was a no-show for his night, so I stayed to help Faith. What the …"

Alder reaches up and locks the door behind him.

Russ continues to scan Alder up and down. When she sees his condition in better light, her expression darkens.

He's disheveled—his coat ripped, dried blood caked over a large goose egg on his forehead. He's barely standing.

"Doc, what happened? Lemme—"

Alder shakes his head and holds up a hand.

Russ lowers her voice. "Power's out. We're on backup. People are either being weird or disappearing! What the hell is going on?"

Alder turns sharply. "In here. C'mon."

Russ's eyes catch the war club in Alder's grip. She stops.

It's glowing.

"Holy—" she breathes. "That's sick!"

Alder grabs Willow's hand. His vision clears.

Things are starting to make sense.

Alder slips in through the triage room, stepping into the main ER.

A chill snakes up his spine as he stares down the hallway—dark, empty, too still. The dim glow of backup lights flickers weakly against the pale beige walls, casting spaced-out islands of shadows.

Then it hits him—that nauseating odor, mixed with rust and citrus.

Faint. But there.

At the central station, Faith sits facing the entrance, like she and Russ had just paused a serious conversation. Alder assumes it's about all the strangeness—because they sure don't look alarmed enough to be talking about the murderous abomination drinking down souls in MorningStar Falls.

Faith perks up when she spots them.

"Hiiii!"

Alder feels them—the flutterbyes.

The relief.

She's safe.

Beautifully safe.

All that he still believed in would collapse if *his* Faith was taken—by that thing.

The perfect, purple presence in his dreams.

He can't bear the nightmare of disappointing her.

So, Alder has kept her close in his slumber but distant while awake. Because those he lets close are the ones he feels damned to lose.

Before he can speak, Willow bolts.

His vision blurs the instant she lets go.

"Aaaagh." It's like a trap snaps shut inside his skull—crushing, inescapable.

The world narrows. The smell vanishes.

Willow barrels into Faith with such force that Faith—halfway to standing—stumbles back into her chair.

"Hi, baby!" Faith says, her cheeks going red.

As if Faith might disappear, Willow clings to her, her face buried in Faith's neck.

Her tiny body shudders—silent at first, then erupting in loud, heartbreaking sobs.

Tears spill hot and fast down Willow's cheeks, soaking into Faith's scrub top.

With a concerned expression, Faith soothes her, gently rocking her while looking up at Alder.

"Ooooh, my sweet, sweet little baby. It's OK, eh."

Alder's pain spikes into searing agony. The weight of his body feels like two pallets of bricks stacked on his shoulders.

Willow loosens her grip on Faith just enough to wipe at her eyes, sniffling.

But the moment she pulls back, her face twists again, and she dives in for another hug, clutching even tighter.

Faith's eyes widen, as if surprised.

The expression on her face shifts, her nose scrunches, but she keeps her body relaxed as she calms Willow.

"It's OK, baby." Faith's voice is sweet, steady. "Hey. Know what I brought? Chocolate chippers. Want one?"

Willow sniffles but nods. Her little tummy does the vocalizing for her.

Russ guides Willow by the shoulders, leading her toward the break room on the far side of the ER.

Willow holds her look of concern, checking on Alder as she walks.

She turns back, but Russ softly guides her away.

"Lets-ago, pun'kin! We'll come back."

Faith stands and wipes tears from her face.

Her soft eyes snap to the lump on Alder's forehead. Dried blood is caked over the swelling and in his hair.

She stammers, her voice thick. "Wh—what happened? What is going on tonight? We can't get in touch with anyone in the hospital … Roland is a no-show … and there's no sign of Sheriff Tom."

Alder doubles over, pinching his forehead.

Faith reaches. "Hey … sit down. Let me take care of you."

Alder interrupts, "Wha—No time for this. Everything is fu—"

"Sit. Down. Alder!" Faith insists. "Talk while I clean you up."

Alder sets the war club on the counter. Its glow fades, and its magical display of light stutters and goes dark, leaving a dull stalk of wood.

Faith frowns and points. "What is—"

The war club reacts as her hand draws near, bursting with vibrance—going dark again as she pulls away.

"That's Sarah." Alder huffs a laugh, but splitting pain quickly replaces his amusement. "Aaaah—shit."

"Let's go over here," Faith says as she leads Alder under the arm to one of the patient rooms. She yanks a curtain open with her free hand.

Alder clenches his eyes shut, trying to block any light from entering—and to keep what's inside from spilling out. That's what it feels like. Like his noodle is feeling around for the nearest opening in his skull to squeeze out.

Faith takes Alder to a cot. She helps lift his legs, then reaches to fling open a cabinet over the sink in the room. She gathers a kidney basin, a large syringe, and a bottle of sterile saline. She sucks up saline with the syringe, then holds the basin against Alder's face with one hand before spraying the water over his abrasion with the other.

Alder jerks. "Shhhhh. Sorry."

"It's OK ... go on," Faith says gently. "What happened?"

Alder exhales a staccato breath. "There's somethin' ... It's killin' everybody, Fai—"

He takes a swallow, and even this makes his head expand. "I saw it—Sheriff—right there—in front of us—ate him ... ate him whole."

Faith stops dabbing at his wound.

"We saw that patient—Mr. Benoit ... and Frank—his son—it killed them too. Right there. Right there in front of us, like it was nothing."

Alder's voice cracks; he stutters, and his lips tremble. "And Mama Curlie. Mama Cur—" Alder's voice wavers and thickens. His eyes go glassy. "She's gone too."

Alder doesn't notice that Faith has stopped cleaning.

She sits back slowly, the kidney basin trembling in her grip. Bloodied water sloshes over the rim. Her eyes flood with tears. Her chin trembles as she gently places the supplies on the counter—her gaze is fixed on the floor.

"Miss Curlie?" Faith whispers.

Alder gives a single, delicate nod—anything more would break open a packet of pain. It's already the worst headache of his life.

"She's gone, Fai—God. S-she—" Alder's eyes shine beneath a pool of tears.

"Alder … what are you saying?" Faith asks, her voice tight.

"Faith! There's a frigg—a monster out there. They called it a Windig—"

"A Windigo?" Faith finishes.

He blinks. "You know it?"

Her breath shudders. "Yes … yeah … I know what that is."

"You saw it—?"

"N-no. It's old folklore … Algonquin. I grew up hearing the stories. But they're just … stories, Alder. A Native boogeyman … to get kids to behave."

With a clumsy lurch, Alder jumps to his feet.

"It killed her—it killed her! Stories? I saw it—I-It …"

His breath collapses. His knees do too. They both give way to the thunderclap of pain in his head.

Alder plummets onto the bed. Faith lunges forward, catching him before he crashes.

"Aaaah. Shit … shit … aaah." His voice is raw, strained.

Faith grips his shoulders, steadying him. "Lie down. Please, just lie down!"

Alder concedes. He slowly lifts his feet and cautiously lies back—

careful not to let the agonizing pain explode into something biblical.

"It's ov—" He doesn't finish his sentence.

Speaking hurts. Even thinking hurts.

As he settles back, his eyes drift upward to the overhead TV.

*   *   *

The TV image flickers in and out—interference from Goodwin, or maybe from Alder's failing vision. Through the static, two words flicker in and out at the bottom of the screen: NASA Spokesperson.

"No, it's unlikely to be a chemical attack—at least, not from any known source on earth," the female speaker says, her voice slightly warbled by interference. "As I mentioned earlier, preliminary analysis of the meteorite samp ... three previously unknown elements ... do not ... to be radioactive ... but ... still assessing their properties—"

The sound cuts out.

Alder stares blankly at the screen. He feels a prickling sensation on his back, like icy fingers tracing his spine.

He jumps up from the cot. "We need to block 'em—the doors— everything, Faith. Please. It's just us now. W-we gotta go. We have to—"

Alder's mind races, sizzling in a hellfire of torture. "This thing. It wants me. We g-gotta go!" He shakes his head, pressing his fingers into his temple.

The room sways. Alder's head pounds, vision tunneling. The tilt wrecks his balance.

Familiar.

Nights of heavy drinking. Drugs.

Tossing his income, dollar by dollar, across the card table.

Pints of booze to wash down benzos and ecstasy.

Cocaine to keep his eyes open just enough to drive—like a frightened centipede veering through Chicago or Las Vegas traffic.

Those years are gone. Still, Alder isn't a lightweight. This is different.

His knees buckle. He drops onto the bed, gripping the edge to steady himself.

The squeak of the call-room door can be heard from beyond the curtain, followed by the pitter-patter of little feet.

Frantically, Willow scrambles to reach Alder's bedside. Faith catches her just as she's about to leap onto the cot, seizing her at the waist.

Faith says, "It's OK, baby girl. I got him."

She signals to Russ to grab Willow.

Gently, Russ takes Willow's hand as she moves to her side. "Yo, hey, pun'kin … let's go make you another cave. Let Faith take care of Dr. P so he can get better. I'll let you play with my Game Boy the whole time, OK?"

Willow hesitates, her eyes fixed on Alder's. He nods, then pleads with his eyes. He doesn't want her to see this.

"I … gonna be OK … go."

She looks down, forces a nod, and allows Russ to guide her to the call room. She wipes her eyes as they walk away. Russ twists the door open, flicking on the light. Willow stands, backlit in the doorway. Her eyes check on Alder one last time before the door clicks shut behind her.

As soon as Willow is gone, Alder exhales a breath he didn't know he was holding. His pain, his guilt, his grief—all of it breaking free, too heavy to contain.

His shoulders tense; his breath quickens. His left hand trembles slightly as he gestures toward the dark screen. He digs deep to speak.

"See—all of dis—it's connected." His voice wavers. "The fuckin' … comet. This thing. Me. Willow. What the fuh— The f— Aaaah!"

He turns to Faith, desperate, searching for an answer he knows she doesn't have.

"Please—you know what it is—wh-what do we … what do we …"

A sharp breath stutters out of him. He drags a hand down his face, fingers pressing into his skin as if trying to ground himself. "It's coming for me, isn't it?"

Faith doesn't answer. But her eyes say enough—questions, fear, something just as unsteady as he feels. She doesn't bear the face of someone with answers.

Alder rocks his head; his body pitches forward on the bed. "It feeds … on the bad shit … that's wh— That's what Benoit said—"

Faith squints. "Mr. Benoit?"

Alder breathes raggedly. His eyes dart to the ceiling as he struggles to focus.

"Yeh—it killed him too."

A dizzying, sickening motion grips him, blurring the room into a chaotic swirl. He's losing himself.

"Ma?" Alder's voice cracks. "M-mama?"

A tear slips down his cheek.

"I swear I didn't know. I should've been there. I was weak. I was lost—" His voice hitches, the words unraveling into something raw. "I was too weak!"

His body curls over, his elbows digging into his knees. His whole frame shudders as his breathing turns into quiet, gasping sobs. "I'm sorry … I'm so sorry."

For a moment, Faith hesitates. Then, slowly, she steps forward.

She kneels beside him, close but not forcing anything. Then, gently, she places her fingers against the back of his neck.

"Hey … I got you, OK?" Her voice is soft, steady.

Alder's body stiffens at first, then he exhales—a long, shuddering breath. He sits up slightly but keeps his eyes closed, embarrassed by his sudden collapse.

"It's OK," Faith soothes.

She guides his head to her chest, her fingers stroking the nape of his neck. She smells good. Lavender, vanilla. For the first time in days, Alder feels something close to relief.

His headache dulls, the tension slipping from his shoulders.

After a long moment, Alder pulls back, his eyes locking onto hers. Faith doesn't move, doesn't let go of his face. For a beat, neither of them speaks.

Then, without thinking, his lips find hers. Soft. Calming. Enough to quiet the beast—not the one stalking Morningstar Falls, but the one raging inside Alder. The energy that surges through him is different from what he felt holding Willow. Both feel restorative, but this soothes rather than jolts. Like tiny hands are inside of him, mending every broken cell.

Her breath catches, but she doesn't pull away. Instead, her hands glide up, fingers cradling his face. The world outside—the Windigo, the pools of blood with no bodies, the effin' comet—all of it blurs into nothing. Faith's tongue sweeps across his, as electrons make a healing dance into his face. This feeling? Bliss.

Alder's heartbeat slows, and for the first time in days, he feels it. He isn't anticipating the next attack. He's not running.

Alder just … is.

The silence between them shifts—deep and warm. Nothing moves except the soft brush of their lips, the quiet rhythm of breath shared in the stillness.

Faith leans in, wrapping her arms around him. Alder's body relaxes as they exhale together, slow and steady.

He feels a surge of relief, then reaches for her face—but he pauses when he remembers her past trauma.

"I'm sorry."

Faith nods softly, takes his hand, and gently places it on the side of her neck. She lets him—offering trust where fear once lived.

They continue to look into each other's eyes. Then Alder's banging headache returns. Faith's beauty fades to a blur in front of him.

He jerks back, shoving Faith away, just as he pukes over the edge of the bed.

"Sorry. I'm—"

"Hey. It's OK," Faith soothes. "C'mon … lie down … please."

She pulls off his coat and guides him back onto the stretcher, raising the head slightly.

Alder's legs feel heavy—especially the left one. He struggles to lift it, so Faith does it for him.

He closes his eyes tightly, his forearm trying to block out more light—and to hold his brain in.

Faith reaches to the wall at the head of the bed, then clicks the light switch. At least it's dark behind Alder's lids now.

"I was weak," Alder says, his voice a brittle scat.

Faith sits down slowly in a chair at the bedside.

"I was weak … I couldn't face her. My mother," he continues. "The gambling, the drugs, and alcohol … I tho-I thought I could get ahead. It all piled up."

He swipes at a tear, but his vision stays blurred. A soft silhouette remains—Faith, listening. Her hand rests lightly on his.

"Alder …" Her voice is quiet, near his ear. "It's OK."

Through the static in his head, it blurs—*Itsa-key.*

Alder cuts her off. "She got sick." He pauses and thumbs at the corner of his weeping eye again. "She got sick, and I couldn't face her. I was a shell … I figured … get my shit together, then get home."

He grimaces. He fails in his futile attempt to stave off breaking down.

"She went quick … gone … it shoulda been … me."

Faith interjects with a soothing and soft, "Shhhhhh."

She stands and kisses Alder's forehead. A soothing current of vigor flows from her lips into his skin—his cells dancing just beneath the surface.

"Try to sleep, OK? I'll be here. I'm not going anywhere."

Alder mumbles, "Ill Win—?"

"I don't understand," she says.

Alder wants to hear "Ill Wind" by Lee Morgan, but he realizes that it's in his car—on the side of the road with a broken axle.

He shakes his head and pushes out, "Nev-mind."

Pain rips through Alder, but it's not just that—his body is slipping from his control. His words and sentences are not forming as intended, even with intense focus.

Faith says, "I'm here, Alder." The emotion in her voice is obvious.

She twists her head, hiding her face from Alder, but it's clear she's hiding tears. She says, "Lie back, OK. I'll be right out here."

Alder nods. He has no strength to protest.

On her way out, Faith draws the pale curtain closed. Beyond it, her chair at the central station scrapes softly against the floor.

The TV stutters back to life in another room. A NASA spokesperson's voice flickers in and out: "… Yes, through an Einstein-Rosen Bridge is—[static]—another term for that is wooorm—still analyzing—in a theoretical case, there could be a phenooooom—ooo—menon—[static]—now known as Echo Entanglement—"

Faith mutes the TV. Alder can make out her sniffing—a moaning cry as he drifts off. He hears her phone dialing.

Beep. Beep. Beep—Beep.

The call fails.

Her silken voice cracks like porcelain as she whispers to herself:

"Miss Curlie … you saved me …" She sniffs. "I'm sorry I couldn't save—"

Her cry rolls to a boil, moans spilling in staccato bursts between ragged breaths.

* * *

The pounding in Alder's head recedes to a low hum. Relief washes over him, but he floats away to the sound of Faith's delicate, yet soul-crushing sobs.

He floats, feeling weightless—like a leaf riding a gentle breeze.

Alder inhales—deep and endless. A breath stretching beyond time, expanding and unspooling into eternity.

A hush settles. A warmth spreads through him—weightless, boundless. Then, movement: a lush, living ripple of green unfurls, as if a gentle hand had placed him in a world that had always been waiting.

Leaves ripple with life, drinking golden light that's cascading in thick, radiant rays.

Alder's being—his essence—feels impossibly small and vast at once. He perceives everything, from the slow dance of leaves in the wind to the quiet alchemy unfolding within them. He is witness to the divine dynamics of existence.

The rays beam down, diving into the foliage. Alder feels it. Then, his self follows the light in, through the leaf's velvet-soft surface.

Down into the intricate lattice of life.

Structures fold upon themselves, filigreed tendrils coiling in endless, luminous spirals. He does not move through them—they move through each other. He is no longer separate from what he sees.

Alder has merged with a rolling current ... pouring forward from a source with seemingly no beginning and no end.

Drifting. Swirling. Dissolving into it all.

And then, a shift. A whisper in the current.

Not a person ... but a surrounding presence of Something.

Not a voice ... but a whispering feeling.

A sublime intonation in the form of enveloping warmth.

She has been waiting for you.

"Mama?" Alder asks.

He doesn't hear his own voice, he feels it.

Go deeper—into the dense tissue of our gift to you.

A rare world among many to cradle this embrace.

Their exhalations become your inhalations. Your exhalations become their inhalations.

They sustain you, as you sustain them.

A tender waltz of being.

Gifts to each other.

Gifts given freely are often gifts taken for granted.

"Mama?

Mother, I am. Of all.

"I'm confused. Of all? Who? What is this?"

Don't ask. Feel. The answers are above you, beneath you, and within you.

Alder feels.

You cannot do this alone.

If you must always try in solitude … then you must accept that you will always fail—alone.

Connection builds. Separation destroys.

Energy is to be given, received … and shared.

Alone, it burns. Alone, it consumes.

Join at your roots. Strengthen your trunks.

Share the fire burning within your conjoined hearts.

Then—

Torch the void.

Illuminate the cold, dark reach of nothing … a place We *cannot go.*

You are not alone … for we have sent you a Good Friend.

Through all of your hardships … all of your losses, you will always have:

A Good Friend.

Look inward, then look outward. They will be there. A hand outstretched …

take it!

A familiar, but more intense surge of energy swells from within Alder. He feels his body re-form as it floats upward.

Alder passes through a soothing, emerald-green cloud: Goodwin's tail.

Glittering packets of light drift toward him, brushing his skin like a mist of prickling warmth—a euphoric cascade.

They pass through him gently. The molecules of his being quiver and dance, resonating with a melodic buzz he feels between his eyes.

Joy, unfiltered.

Love, limitless and engulfing.

Peace, so steady it feels motionless.

But peace is not passive. And never still.

It marches with a mightier step than the boots of any army.

Its course often invisible to worldly eyes—yet forever in motion, even in times of strife.

This moment is fragrant to smell, sweet to taste, harmonic to hear, electric to feel, and radiant to see.

It is life.

But in our lives, we have become anosmic, deaf, numb, and blind ... severed connections with frayed, reaching ends.

I love you, Aldi.

The moment of acceptance is the height of all relief. When the chains of fear and grief loosen and fall at your feet. The moment those stilled feet can resume their peaceful march.

"I love you," Alder feels. He surrenders. "I'm ready."

Something yanks Alder backward—suddenly. A violent suction. The warmth vanishes, and he suddenly feels the cold zooming toward him, surrounding him. He feels air hunger take over, but he can't exhale to let a new breath in.

He claws at the warmth, tries to hold on, but it slips through him— like water through thirsty, cupped hands.

Alder fights.

Now this is familiar—the fight.

The fight we all face daily. Just to exist.

He plummets through darkness—silent and empty at first. But soon, he senses a morose presence, waiting.

The darkness deepens. The insidious presence lurks, following him— closing in as the last bit of light and warmth snuffs out.

Nothing.

Not even a pinpoint of light.

Nothing.

No joy. No grief.

No satisfaction. No disappointment.

Not even blackness.

Just pitch.

Nothing.

They can't come here.

He is in this no-place, in this nothingness ... alone.

A voice cuts through the cold vacuum, seizing Alder's heart.

It's his mother's voice.

"Aldi ... my baby boy."

Alder can now feel tears press against his eyes. They throb and ache in their orbital prisons, but refuse to fall.

Nina Graham's Bajan accent obliterates the forbidding silence.

"My little light of mine ... with you, there ain't never no darkness."

The pressure. Alder tries to speak, but the words don't come. He can't hear the rest of her words.

No matter ... he feels them.

The fight we all fight.

Huuuuuuggggh.

Alder jerks awake. His breath explodes from him, as if he'd been holding it for an eternity.

The pain expands in his head like a shaken can of soda. The world tumbles. His eyes dart side to side, and his stomach rises like a balloon.

Alder's mouth fills with saliva. He tries to swallow, but a backward pressure builds. He turns his body over the edge of the bed and vomits again, emptying more than his insides should have had room to hold.

Faith's silhouette scrambles toward the curtain. She pauses just outside—wiping her face, then softly blowing her nose before pulling it aside.

The light of the ER follows her in.

The room tilts violently. Alder's feet feel as if they belong over his head, and then back to the ground again—as if they no longer know their own position in space.

He nearly topples off the bed, but Faith hooks a hand under his arm, yanking him back. He fights to appear strong, to hide the weakness—or at least to carry his own weight.

I'm dying, he thinks.

Sweat and tears drip from the tip of his nose, the brine on his lips reminding him he's still alive.

Every motion stokes the infernal flame raging behind his eyes.

Faith whispers, "I'm here, love … you have to lie back."

She places her soft palm at the base of Alder's head, guiding him down.

A feeling rip-roars down his neck—too fast to even describe.

His vision sharpens for a beat, revealing a clearer image of Faith's flushed face and eyes—tears spill down her soft cheeks.

Then—like a forgotten memory bubbling to the surface—a realization flashes:

Is this what John Benoit saw?

Willow—we're not just connected. We're the same. She's me … but from another place. Another time.

A place where Donkey Kong and the ketchup are different.

"Wil—aaagh!" Alder's rasp is cut short by agony. "Where … Willow?"

Faith replies, "Alder, lie down. She's in the call room. You don't want her to see this, OK, love? Lie down."

At close range, Alder sees the rawness of her face and the deep, puffy redness around her eyes. Evidence of the crying he'd heard.

"I c-can't! We got to—together—"

He tries to rise, but his legs fail him, and he spills back onto the bed.

"We gotta be close. That thing ... coming ... dammit!"

"DR. P!" Faith's voice cuts through the room.

Alder freezes. He looks up and sees her face. Faith's beautiful, teary face. Two of them.

"Faith ... the vision. L-like Benoit said. That monster ... it wants to destroy us ... it can't when we-together—"

He shakes his head, gripping his temples. "I think ... hell am I saying?"

Faith grips the bedrail with pale knuckles. She plucks her handheld phone from her side, fingers trembling as she dials.

Erastus, the CT tech, speaks through the receiver.

"CT."

Faith answers with a rare edge of urgency.

"We need this scan. Now."

A pause.

"I mean ... we can try."

Faith shakes her head.

"We're coming—even if I have to stand in there and hand crank it!"

She exhales sharply and hangs up.

"I'm taking you myself."

Alder feels himself slipping again as he hears a muffled, *wheeaaaaarrrraahhrrrrr.*

Faith doesn't seem to notice.

"F-F-Fai—"

He can't fight the words out: *Go—ple—go. All-you. H-hide.* His mind speaks, but his tongue doesn't.

Tears trail into his ears, like rivers returning to the sea. But even with the dam broken, the pressure behind his eyes won't relent.

He shuts them to darkness, tinged pink by the blood pulsing behind his lids.

CHAPTER EIGHT

Alder comes to, disoriented at first, but the rhythmic rattle of his hospital cot and the light reflecting off the muted green walls slowly bring him back to reality.

Faith is at the head of the bed, pushing it down the mostly dark hallway toward the CT scan suite. It's not a long hallway, but to Alder, it's the length of a bumpy football field.

Backup lights flicker overhead—spaced too far apart—leaving stretches of darkness.

She smells good. Like a sunny Saturday morning in spring.

Serene. Safe.

Her delicate face sharpens in his vision, followed by the slow sway of her ID badge ticking in front of her locket. Alder watches it: tick-tock, tick-tock—until the world tilts and his nausea swells.

He squeezes his eyes shut and turns his head—

A searing shockwave explodes inside, forcing a gasp.

It's like a pickaxe through the center of his forehead ... his brain groping for that exit.

Faith glances down.

When Alder blinks his eyes open, her soft brown gaze finds his and holds it.

Her voice drapes over the pain.

"We're almost there."

She plucks up her hospital cordless and dials.

Beep, beep, beep. Beep.

A faint ring drifts through the quiet hallway as Faith holds the phone to her ear, guiding the bed with her other hand.

Blurry ceiling stains zip by above. Each jostle of the stretcher's wheels sends vibrations through Alder, accompanied by stray drafts brushing his forehead.

"No one's—ugh …" Faith's grip tightens on the phone. "Where the hell is Jennings? Where is anyone?"

Beep.

She dials another four numbers.

Boop, boop. The call fails.

"Dammit! Still can't dial out either."

She slips the phone back into her scrubs pocket and grips the bed with both hands, swinging it left down a narrower hallway. Despite his washed-out sight, Alder recognizes the glow of the signs ahead.

CT IN USE. DO NOT ENTER.

Faith bangs on the shielded door with the side of her fist. The knock is dull, swallowed by thick metal.

A loud clunk. The lock disengages.

The door swings inward.

Erastus, the stocky Greek CT tech, stands hunched, as if bracing for something.

Dark hairs at the back of his neck poke out from his scrubs collar. His face barely registers Alder's stretcher as it rolls past him.

"CT head—without contrast?" Erastus asks.

"Without, right, Alder?" Faith confirms.

Alder starts to nod, but pain stops him halfway.

"We'll see if there's enough juice," Erastus says. "Generators might not hold." He exhales, shrugging his shoulders. "It's just a head scan, so … maybe."

* * *

The humming scanner. The smell of new plastic hangs in the air.

This CT machine was gifted to MFMC by a wealthy donor two years ago, but doesn't get as much use in a hospital this *quiet*.

Alder knows this room.

The narrow table—walkways on either side. The cold sterility of it all.

The stretcher turns, then stops.

He smells Faith to his right.

Erastus to his left—cheap musk from a green bottle. Too much.

"One, two, three."

They slide Alder onto the firmer surface.

"Ah—ah—stop. Just stop," Alder pleads.

Straps tighten over his chest. Velcro rips, securing him in place.

Faith's voice brushes his right ear, low and reassuring.

"I'll be right in there …"

She kisses his forehead, and warmth ripples above his eyebrows but fades as soon as her soft lips lift away.

As Faith moves into the control room, her dainty footsteps whisper away. She and Erastus stand behind shielded glass, just outside the scan room.

The room goes dark. Alder can perceive that much.

The scanning table creaks softly as it glides upward, guiding Alder headfirst into the machine. A bright-red beam sweeps over his closed eyelids, leaving a phantom glow in its wake.

A synthetic female voice cuts through the static hum, cocooning him from the neck up.

"Hold still … now … please remain still … now … please remain still …"

It repeats. Again. And again.

The words stretch, bending time into something unrecognizable.

Then—a loud crash.

It comes through the door at Alder's feet, from just outside the CT suite, folded into the droning commands still emanating from the machine circling his head.

"Hold still ... hold still ..."

Finally, the scan ends. The machine cycles down, yawning like a tired animal.

The table slides Alder out of the ring, chin first.

From the control room, Faith's distant voice reaches him.

"... You think it's an epidural?"

Erastus's reply is flat. Matter-of-fact.

"Yeah ... I'll try to send it to the radiologist, but yeah. On the right. It's shifting his brain."

Alder knows what this means.

An epidural hematoma: bleeding between his brain and skull.

It explains everything.

His slipping grip on consciousness.

Why his vision flickers in and out.

Even the false improvement.

It's called the *Lucid Interval.*

A false dawn. A fragile window of improvement that leads to dangerous complacency.

The illusion that the injury isn't severe—while the bleeding builds in silence, and the brain is slowly pushed off-center.

Now ...

His body won't obey.

And his speech is slipping.

He'd even had those stuttering moments of clarity—hallucinations, maybe—thinking Willow's touch had something to do with his recovery.

Ha!

Head injuries.

Recovery.

But still, what about—

Faith returns to Alder's right side from the control room. He tilts his head toward her heavenly scent—longing to hear that angelic voice.

It soothes him—always.

No matter the words. No matter the situation.

Through the glass, Erastus punches buttons.

With the whooshing sound of all power shutting down, the room is plunged into darkness.

"Shit. Well—we used it all up. Give it a minute," Erastus huffs.

Alder hears and feels Faith still at his right side in the dark.

She says, "He-hey. I'm he—"

Just as serenity pours into his ears, an explosive noise cuts her off as the shielded CT suite door rips from its hinges. It crashes with a deafening racket against the wall across the hall. The sound is like a stick of dynamite in Alder's brain.

Air rushes out. The dull flicker of the hallway backup sconces spills in.

A massive, shadowed form looms beyond the wreckage. The Windigo.

Its body writhes—eel-like appendages lashing and twitching, its wide spray of jagged antlers silhouetted against the stuttering hallway lights.

It tears the door off like it was made of cardboard.

The Windigo drops onto all fours.

Thumph.

Pain shreds through Alder's pressurized brain, but he rolls onto his side to look. The backup lights pair with his blurred vision, casting gray and muted shadows at his feet.

The monster's fiery blue eyes scan the room as it squeezes through the doorway, its massive, twisted antlers scraping the frame—snapping off splintered tips as it forces its way inside.

It enters the CT suite slowly. Deliberately.

Then—

The bright lights snap back on, illuminating Erastus in the control room, frozen behind the glass.

Alder can't see his face. But he sees his chest expand in a panicked, irregular rhythm.

The Windigo's head twists toward the control room in a slow, smooth motion. Erastus stumbles backward until he is against the control room wall, cornered. His breath shudders. Just as he screams out—

It slams into the control room in a blur, antlers shattering against the frame—making straight for the nearest body: Erastus.

A wet, sickening pickle-snap.

A croaking cry, cut down into a faint wheeze.

A whimper, snapped short as blood spatters across the glass, leaving a ruby-red tint.

Alder crashes to the floor.

Faith falls while trying to catch him. Her head slams against the wall, a sharp crack echoing in the sudden silence. Her body tenses, just before going limp.

Alder tries to cry out. "Ffff—"

His tongue won't obey.

The bleeding between his brain and skull compresses his brain. This much he knows; he heard it all.

He tries to stand, but only one leg responds.

Alder drags himself along the floor toward Faith, who lies motionless.

The Windigo emerges from the control room, drenched in blood— its wormy skin drinking in the gore, just as before. Gray, writhing worms, slick with slime, twist beneath its flesh, chasing one another in frantic loops. As they agitate, a stringy, pink-tinged goo bubbles up and squirts from its body.

Its cold-infernal eyes clear the doorframe, fixed intently on Alder.

It thumps forward on its razor-sharp feet—stalking toward Faith without breaking eye contact with Alder.

The Windigo doesn't pulverize her like it did Erastus. Instead, it reaches down, seizes her leg, and hurls her into the dimly lit hallway. Her scent vanishes, swallowed by the creature's own vile stench as her body slams into the far wall.

Faith doesn't even a moan. Just a sickening crack, echoing back—proof that something deep inside has shattered.

Rage—raw, unfiltered, and absolute—consumes Alder.

He claws forward, dragging himself across the cold floor.

A razored hand seizes the back of his neck.

Fire erupts down his spine as the claws rip through his flesh.

The Windigo drags Alder into the hallway, his limp body dangling from its grip—held by the neck, like a cat with wounded prey. It stops at Faith, and with its other hand, picks her up and suspends her body in front of Alder.

It lifts him higher. Face to face. While looking directly into his eyes, the monster hurls her farther down the long corridor.

His vision is failing—but not nearly enough.

Up close, it's worse.

Unspeakably grotesque in every sense.

Its long, sinewy face twitches.

Jagged, knifelike teeth jut from the empty spaces of its stretched maw. Its eyes—impossibly blue flames—are light itself, desperate to escape, running toward reality only to be swallowed by nothing.

They are gateways.

Alder sees through them, into something vast and ever-consuming.

No heat radiates from its body. Instead, it drinks the warmth from Alder's skin, siphoning it away.

Its stench is beyond death. It smells of a rot left to fester over millions of years.

A ghostly vapor lifts from Alder's face.

He sees it in his periphery—photons of light struggling to return to him.

But they don't.

They drift toward the creature's flaring nostrils, caught in its pull. Swallowed.

Consumed by the infernal vacuum within its chest.

Between his own body and this space, Alder can feel himself being stretched.

Nearing the bowels of the Windigo, Alder can feel, not hear, the distorted screams of others.

This thing is not hate.

It's something worse.

Indifference.

Greed, laced with apathy.

All of the warmth and light—the care, the love—pours into this sick, slithering thing.

Snuffed out by … nothing.

Its pain is unquenchable—because it's pain that feeds itself.

He stares down the creature's gaping mouth, then closes his eyes.

Alder didn't turn away out of apathy, but shame—it swallowed him whole.

Her doctor son—he couldn't even save her when she lost her home. She paid the student debt she cosigned for, all while sacrificing her own expenses.

His money went down the drain, but she never knew.

Or did she?

When she fell ill, he couldn't face her because he was sicker.

Addiction.

Gambling was just a piece of it. She hated it, but Alder had worse vices. How could he face her?

He had nearly lost his hospital privileges, showing up to a shift drunk in Chicago. Thankfully, he had an understanding director—discreet.

She got him the help. It took a while for him to take it.

When he did, it was too late.

Gone before that first night away in rehab, before the first meeting.

His mother died of cancer while he hid, from her.

When she needed him the most, he had tried to protect himself.

Sobriety sharpens guilt.

It peels back the insulation. Forces you to see how your presence—or absence—has impacted those you love.

It's a guilt that eclipses the shame of intoxication itself.

You atone—if you're lucky.

If not, you become Alder Peony.

The guilt only compounds with time, and you beg for your time to come.

A pain that feeds upon itself.

A sick, slithering thing.

Like the Windigo.

Pressure builds behind Alder's closed lids. It burns. It pains. But allowing the tears to spill won't relieve any of it.

An even stronger pressure clamps down in his chest. A phantom claw wrenches and macerates his heart.

It squeezes. Tightening, puncturing, sinking deeper.

His heart leaks the force that makes it beat, but before Alder slips into the deepest dark, a light explodes—from a pinhole to a brilliance that washes out all else.

Soft and tranquil.

His father's love and protection.

The sisters at the group home who carried it forward.

As did his adoptive mother, Nina Graham—the only mother he'd ever known.

Glimpses of loss come and go, but love is steady and unwavering, crystallized in new bonds.

Willow.

Her emerald-green eyes, grinning—dancing—pumping her tiny, raised fist to Kanye West.

Faith.

Scarred by life, yet still holding to her mission of smiles.

It builds.

He feels it.

Love is the hand that reaches for you through the gloaming.

It reaches—for love.

For love—is the light itself.

Take it!

Alder reaches.

He fights.

But his body won't react.

The fire is there.

The will burns.

But the flesh is sopping with despair.

A cold shell at its bitter end. Trapped in the darkest void of nothingness.

A place *She* cannot go, but they can.

A fiery shine glows on the wall—coming from behind Alder. A deep, humming vibration.

Then …

A thunderous crack splits the air, followed by a burst of white-hot light. Even with his eyes squeezed shut, Alder's brain feels like it's come to a rolling boil—bubbling behind his ears, rising and dipping like eggs in a saucepan.

The sound reverberates through the hallway, fading into a deafening rattle.

The walls tremble. Painted mortar dust trickles from between the bricks.

The Windigo's antlers whip backward as Alder crashes face-first to the floor.

The Ojibwe war club—Sarah—tumbles beside his cheek.

Clop. Clop. Clop.

The Windigo reels back. Its antlers rip through the ceiling tiles, sending down a cascade of dust and jagged debris.

A cut-off cry as it hits the floor—

The sound—like a ton of bundled jelly slapping tile.

Its grotesque form sprawls across the narrow hallway.

Its body is so large that its neck flexes against one wall, and its clawed feet scrape the opposite.

The slithering appendages infesting its body convulse—writhing, extending, and snapping back in restless spasms.

A faint glow from Sarah illuminates Alder's closed eyelids.

A surge of warmth floods his shoulders—where the war club lies.

It's Russ. She used it against the thing.

Her voice is distant, muffled—but she's right there, pulling at him, dragging him toward safety.

"Doc ... come ... on!"

Her hands clamp onto his legs. One yank. Then another.

She ratchets him through the ED doors in four earnest heaves—each one a fight—hauling him away from the fallen monster.

The doors slam shut just as the creature moves.

Its appendages twitch—squirm restlessly like a barrel full of gray, mucus-drenched snakes.

Faith lies motionless.

Out there.

At the end of the same hallway.

A cloudy bundle of purple in the distance.

The Windigo stands between them and her.

Alder, still on the floor, leans toward the door—then buckles onto his side.

He's trying to reach Faith.

The automatic doors hiss open.

Russ yanks him back, propping him against a supply cart.

"Doc! Please!"

She reaches up but can't quite reach the shutoff switch. Alder focuses on her rainbow socks—bobbing up and down like tubes of fun, streaking color through his blurred vision.

They're trapped on stage between two black curtains at the edges of his sight.

It takes him to the edge of giggling.

Oh, rasshole, Aldi! You've finally lost your shit.

"W-w-w—"

Alder can't get Willow's name out.

She needs to be near. The creature will retreat—or at least hesitate.

"W-w—Pl-p—" *Please understand me.*

Russ leans closer. "Willow?"

Alder nods.

"She's in the call room—I locked it."

A thump comes from the call room—knocking and the frantic jostling of the doorknob.

"Please! Please! Dr. P!" Willow's voice cracks. "Russ!"

Alder tries again. Faith is hurt.

"F-f-f-f-fai—"

The words won't come.

Russ gets face to face with him. "Where's Faith?"

Alder's tongue still doesn't obey.

Russ crawls toward the automatic door, but it doesn't open. She yanks it manually.

Both doors slam open laterally, and Russ winces.

"Shit!" she mutters. "Where did it go?"

She sticks her head into the hallway—just enough to see.

Her breath catches.

"Is that Faith?"

Scrambling up, Russ snatches the no-longer-glowing Sarah

from the floor.

Russ bolts through the door, her rainbow socks streaking through Alder's sight.

Her Chucks squeak on the linoleum.

Then, a sickening sound echoes down the hallway.

The unmistakable thud of flesh against force—her shoe-squeak silenced. A second slapping sound—flesh against a wall—followed by dead silence.

The war club tumbles to the floor, rolling to a stop.

Clop-clop-clop.

Alder's vision tilts. He begs for the strength to get down the hallway—to help Faith and Russ. At this point, he'd settle for being a sacrifice. He trembles, feeling like a prisoner in a bundle of flesh, trapped within his own useless body.

He's crying. He feels the tears, but his face remains flat.

He opens his mouth. No words.

Instead, a raw, primal sound rips from his throat.

"MMMMMMWWWAAAAH—"As if this would scare the Windigo off.

From the hallway comes the sound of slow, wet footsteps.

The stench follows.

Oranges. Rust. Putridity.

With his right arm, Alder drags himself forward, inch by inch, toward the doorway between the hall and the ER.

His neck kinks as he pulls himself along.

His head presses to the floor.

He uses it too.

With half of his limbs not functioning, he tries to use anything to propel himself forward.

The mechanical door slams into his ribs repeatedly, pushing the breath from his lungs. Every three seconds.

Three seconds.

Again.

Three seconds.

Again.

Three. Seconds.

He turns his head. His double vision swims. He can see the blurred coloration of Russ's rainbow socks, her motionless legs jutting from around the corner of the adjoined hallway. Alder blinks—tries to focus—but they remain motionless.

The Windigo lumbers toward him. Its malodorous smell crescendos in intensity as it approaches.

Sh-thumph ... sh-thumph ... sh-thumph.

It's holding Faith.

Purple scrubs. Limp. Dangling from its grip.

Alder blinks, and the blurred purple figure of Faith squirms in the Windigo's massive grasp.

The vile thing squeezes her, no, crushes her.

It sounds like a bundle of dry twigs being wrenched, twisted—

Her face, a mask of pain, doesn't match the pitiful whimper from her lips.

Alder's sight improves only to witness the most horrific thing.

A grimace, born of unimaginable pain, distorts her beautiful face— the worst thing he's seen yet. Her cheek dimple now stretched, pulling— not winking at Alder.

Unlike the blushing grin she wore while cutting Willow's blueberry pancakes. Or her head tilting as she watched the little girl play with her food.

It's not the look she has when the crew raves over her baking.

This expression, Alder can barely stomach.

He doesn't need full vision to see those ghastly blue flames for eyes.

He can feel them.

Its eyes fix on Alder. With direct eye contact, the creature's razored hand slowly moves and traces down Faith's right forearm, flaying open her soft skin.

Faith screams like a weak lamb.

Why doesn't it just swallow her whole?

It seems to savor every second of Alder's torment.

It is torturing him. It'll have a good feeding from the rage and hate brewing inside of Alder by the time it's done. Maybe that's its goal. Maybe the ultimate feast is him. Maybe it has been the whole time—all of its hope placed in fattening up his inner demon so that it's finally fulfilled, and the Windigo can quench its own pain.

And Alder—

He deserves every bit.

Faith? Willow? Russ? Mama Curlie? Sheriff Tom?

They don't deserve to suffer for his vices—his failures.

He must pay the price for those—he alone must atone.

Slowly, the Windigo's huge hand tightens its grip around Faith's throat. It appears like it's being careful not to cut her.

It must know about her trauma. It knows—and it's feeding on it.

Faith shakes her head, her breath trembling.

Tears spill from her big brown eyes—both nearly swollen shut.

She whimpers, "N-n-no."

With her right hand, Faith paws helplessly at the monster's grip. Her other arm twitches and flaps uselessly at her side.

She gasps. The monster's grip cinches tighter.

Her locket, her cherished locket, snaps loose and falls to the floor like loose change.

The Windigo doesn't even look at her.

It watches Alder intently. He can feel those eyes piercing him.

Faith's brown eyes make contact with Alder's. Her swollen cheeks soaked with tears. A weak moan escapes her lips, as if she is trying to speak her final words—her eyebrow lifts, then dips into a frown as the monster tightens its grip around her delicate neck.

All the while, the Windigo doesn't take its eyes off of Alder, its head tilted.

"P-pl-agh-agh-AAAAAAH." Alder can't get his plea out. As if he could garner some mercy from the malignant being from nowhere.

Rage engulfs Alder, but the weight of his helplessness tempers it— both so immense they eclipse even the pain splitting his head.

Alder flings his right arm. It flaps against the floor. He tries to pull himself up, but his body refuses.

He digs in and tries again, but his head flops to the side like a newborn's.

Alder's spirit burns, it is afire, but his body is a cold, half-dead failure.

His desire to grab the Windigo by the throat and twist until its blue-fire eyes go dark grows stronger. But he can't.

He alone isn't enough.

All he can do is claw at the cold linoleum, inch by inch. To sit up and die facing it—or die ass-up on the speckled white floor.

The Windigo hurls Faith again, like discarded trash, not even watching. She skids and rolls—vanishes into shadow. A muffled halt. Her legs jut out of the darkness, twisted at unnatural angles.

The creature shoves Alder against the painted brick wall, pinning him upright. His head tips back on his limp neck.

Alder's eyes widen as the immense thing looms over him. Its snot-eel appendages lash, flinging swill strings into the air.

With his failing vision, the things look like the sea at dusk— undulating, rippling with a sickening motion.

Alder has nothing left.

No fight.

No deus ex machina.

Just the quiet surrender of a man who, if given the choice, would trade his life for the rest of them. There's not much of that life left anyway. Not much good behind it, either. So why hold fast to it? Why toil to salvage something of no worth?

Perhaps there is worth in his sacrifice.

Maybe the abomination will leave everyone else alone after getting its fill—and there's plenty there. Maybe enough.

Though Alder won't be here to know it.

Alder thought he could escape here. Vanish into some tree-covered corner of the country. Hide from the selfish, neglectful thing he used to be.

But this—this is where his reckoning was always waiting.

The Windigo watches him—waiting too—as it pins his slack body against the wall.

Alder prays silently. Not for a miracle. Just for his end.

Acceptance ...

But this time, it reeks of decay and tortured surrender.

The fuck are you waiting for?

TAKE IT!

Quench your vile hunger and move the FUCK ON!

You foul bundle of nothing.

NOW ... DAMMIT!

"N-no-dab f-f-ooo."

He would scream that if he could, but only a whimper escapes his lips.

A wet and coarse sound grinds through the air, like damp gravel in a throat long dead.

Kuh-kuh-kuh.

It sounds like laughter.

It's taunting him.

The creature drops Alder to the floor. He falls under the weight of his own body, like a two-hundred-pound sack of meat.

Then it slams down onto its forelimbs with a thud that rattles the floor—sending a quake through Alder's skull, jostling his already compressed mind and leaving behind the faint, metallic tang of blood.

His light is fading, the edges of his vision swallowed by waving shadow—cold, silent. A flash—his mother's face, tears brimming as she watches him cross the stage at his med school graduation. Her voice, warm as an ember. He hears her now.

"Go do what you're meant to do, son. I never knew your father, but I thank him every day—I thank him for my Aldi. I am so proud of you. My little light … my only true pride!"

Something catches. A spark. A fuse ignites deep inside him.

A blinding eruption of green light engulfs everything. It doesn't burn. It doesn't sear. It drenches. A warmth that reaches through bone floods his chest, his skull, his ribs, his marrow.

The light swells, expanding and stretching through the corridors.

The universe holds its breath.

The walls tremble.

Building.

A pressurizing swell of air.

A second burst—brighter than the first. A bolt of green light.

Pulsing—

Two.

Three times—

The windows shatter inward. Doors rip from their hinges. The hospital groans, as if the fabric of reality itself is being wrenched apart—like the universe just let go—a painful, held breath now bursting free.

Cold rushes in. Frost curls in the seams of the walls.

Shards of glass, splinters of wood—frozen midair. Suspended. The explosion leaves behind an echoing-in-seashell sound.

Glass pieces chime against each other, but they don't harm Alder.

Then the air thickens around him, and a submerged silence hushes the world.

Alder floats in place, weightless. He feels like a fly trapped in a bottle of corn syrup. Down the corridor, Faith's body rises and floats too, her limbs hanging slack.

The Windigo stands frozen, but its feet are still planted to the floor. Only its eyes move—those blue, flaming orbits flicking up and down Alder, pausing at his chest, then slowly rising to meet his eyes. They blaze brighter, blinding him so that all he can see is that light.

Faith's body falls too—but soft as a feather. Limp and light ... like something already gone, her soma cradled with quiet reverence and entrusted to peace itself. The peace her battered body never knew in life.

The monster reaches out. One clawed hand seizes Alder's throat. There's no warmth, no cold, just a drawing void ... draining Alder. A force siphoning the last of him as he slumps against the wall.

Then.

A whisper ... close to his left ear.

"Dr. P ... I'm here."

Two tiny hands grasp his arm firmly.

His breath catches. He can speak.

"Willow?"

The explosion ripped the doors away ... she must have gotten out of the call room, which was locked for her protection.

She got out.

Thank *Something* she got out.

She came to protect him.

With her touch, raw power explodes—outward and inward. It chases itself like a restless green aura.

It's like his vision of floating through Goodwin's tail. Like when he is near Faith, but stronger. Empowering and renewing.

The current loops between Alder and Willow—a shared universal path of electrons, no longer governed by uncertainty but anchored in absolutes.

A living circuit.

An *entanglement*.

A connected puzzle that scrambles the beast.

The Windigo's burning eyes flicker.

It hesitates.

Something shifts inside Alder. Not in his limbs, not in his body—but deeper. A force stirs, rising.

This time, the connection feels unbreakable.

His senses return, and his vision becomes more acute.

Willow clings to him, her arms wrapped around his neck. She scrambles forward, pressing herself between him and the creature— shielding him as if her small body could hold the thing back. It can … and it has.

She buries her face into Alder's neck, her breath quick and uneven with fear.

And then … a supernova ignites inside of Alder, raw and absolute. A force that has been waiting for him. It blasts outward—breaking free—flooding every cell with renewed strength. A burning sensation scatters from his center.

The Windigo staggers back.

Alder rises—steady, unshaken—holding Willow tightly.

The monster lunges. But with every step it takes toward them, its grotesque appendages begin to slough off, melting into the floor and liquefying into vile, putrid sludge.

It reaches for them, desperate. But something holds it back.

Its body jerks, stuttering in place. Glitching. Like it's being rejected by reality itself.

It can't attack them as long as they … *stay together … always.* Willow's mantra.

Snarling, the Windigo rears onto its hind legs, and its antlers rip through the last of the drop ceiling panels. The aluminum frames twist, snap apart; the exposed ductwork slices open.

A radiant current holds the beast at bay, like an ethereal electric fence.

The Windigo's agitation heightens. It belts out a shrill, earsplitting shriek. The air visibly ripples from the otherworldly pressure.

Alder squeezes his eyes shut and tucks his neck. Willow holds her breath and holds tighter.

The sheer magnitude of the noise should knock Alder and Willow flat—at least deafen them—but the sound bends around them both, like a storm breaking against an unseen barrier.

He tightens his grip on Willow, holding her against his chest … as Sarah blazes at the edge of his vision.

Down the hallway next to Faith.

Sarah's glow clings to Faith's swollen face, illuminating the rise and fall of her labored breaths. The fingers on her right hand rise and tremble—small, fragile movements.

She's still alive!

Alder quickly lowers Willow and grips her hand.

It can't reach them when they stand together. Alder is strongest when they stand together.

So, together, they step toward Sarah and Faith—unafraid.

The Windigo slashes at the air … then stops.

Its slithering appendages tense, reaching, their ends glowing a deep, searing red—the burn intensifies.

The stench—rot, decay, death—floods the corridor like a suffocating blanket.

The creature surges forward, lunging.

The current between Alder and Willow begins to thin. Doubt slithers in. He gets a better look at Faith, battered and broken. His sense of failure simmers up.

No use to anyone.

Guilt floods his veins. He feels it sink deep into his core, washing away his tether to Willow.

Cold. Dark. Alone.

Reality fades, eclipsed by the false world his despair has built—a world where he's alone, and always was.

His left knee wobbles. His breath quickens. His vision wavers again but is not completely lost. Enough to see Russ's socks still at the edge of the hall, and Faith just ahead.

Suddenly, Alder's body whips backward.

It found a way through.

The Windigo's claws close around his shoulder and along the base of his neck—a deep, slicing pain shoots into the back of his head.

Alder's strength falters. Slowly, he feels the strength dribble away from his muscles. His vision doubles.

He feels Willow's hand slip—torn from his grip. Cold air floods between their fingers. His whole body lurches forward as he tries to reach her—too slow. Too late. He can't even lift his left arm to reach her; it has gone dead again.

Her hair whips past his face as the Windigo dismissively flings her down the dark hallway opposite them.

Willow's tiny body flies into the darkness, landing somewhere in the distance with a hollow thud.

Blackness creeps in, not just into Alder's vision but into his very existence.

The tether has been severed. To Willow, to Faith, and to this life.

He is alone.

Sarah dims, now a lifeless wood heirloom. Faith's still face is no longer lit, as it fades into the darkness too.

Alder hears Faith's weak moan in his right ear—his left, pressed against the cold floor, hears the machine-work from the lower level beneath the ground floor.

He lies there, feeling his life slip away like a fish that leapt from its tank—regretful, gasping, and forgotten on the linoleum.

* * *

Alder is face down again, struggling for air. The strength that flowed through him moments ago is gone—snuffed out as quickly as it came. His body refuses to move, crushed under the weight of its own failure.

The Windigo plants a foot on his back. Pressing, squeezing, forcing the breath from his lungs.

The creature's scream tears through the air.

Alder sees movement—a blonde-haired silhouette creeping toward him. Her face comes into the light.

Willow.

Army-crawling. Reaching for him.

The barest brush of her fingertips grazes his scalp.

Something stirs. A charge rises inside—not enough to stand, not enough to throw the beast off—but enough to breathe.

Like breaking the surface after drowning, he sucks in air with a gasp.

The Windigo presses its twisted foot harder into his back, crushing Alder's chest against the floor.

Willow pulls herself closer, inching. She reaches out and secures Alder's shoulders. As she makes contact, a vigor rips through him.

The Windigo wobbles as Alder pushes up. It staggers.

This isn't enough to win.

But it's enough to fight.

Alder's eyes lock onto Willow's—green and shining. She's stretched out on the floor, arms still reaching for him.

Her fingers dig into his shoulders, her small hands gripping like a vice. Her face twists, every muscle clenched as if this is the hardest she has ever held onto anything in her life. Her eyes squeeze shut.

Then, something behind Alder catches her attention. The air sizzles.

Willow's eyes snap open. A glow reflects in them.

The light flickers—bobbing up and down. A beacon. Approaching.

She squints. Then, a smirk makes her grimace unwind. Her fingers loosen, just slightly. Tears well up in her eyes as the smirk stretches into a smile.

A sharp crack splits the air as the club swings, driving its ball end against the monster's face.

The Windigo slams into the wall, limbs splaying wide, claws raking deep furrows into the surface.

With a disgusting, wet-sounding splatter, its body hits the floor.

From its midsection, gray, glistening tendrils burst outward—writhing like severed nerves, twitching with live-wire spasms, and oozing thick, stringy, mucus-like streams.

The pressure on Alder's back vanishes. He rolls over.

It's Faith.

She grips Sarah tightly in one hand, the war club pulsing with light.

She holds her side with the other, but slowly stands as if she's healed from the inside out.

Faith looks as strong as Alder feels now—with Willow holding onto him.

The Windigo screeches, its hooked claws raking the ground and dragging itself upright with a sound like nails on a chalkboard.

Faith steadies herself. She grips the war club like a cricket bat. She glances at the glow and nods once, approving. She's here—fully in this moment.

She rears back and swings.

The war club smashes into the Windigo's jaw. Its teeth shriek against the sacred wood carved by the hands of Mr. Benoit, but they don't leave even a scratch on it.

The impact whips its head sideways.

Its antlers slam the walls, fracturing. Jagged shards explode outward, scattering in every direction.

The Windigo twists violently.

Its torso lurches one way, its legs the other. The two halves of its body twist, sliding over each other like melted wax.

It clambers to its feet. Stumbles once.

Suddenly, the monster lunges in a wild, unbalanced charge. Its weight barrels into Faith, hurling her against the wall. It flails against the impact, hitting the wall as well.

The monster crashes down, thrashing, its limbs ensnarled in its own wormy appendages.

Schlop, schlop.

Faith plants her feet without even stumbling.

Whatever power Alder gained from Willow's touch, from Faith's kiss, is nothing compared to what's flowing through her now.

She stands toe to toe with something inhuman, channeling might from another place.

A dry chuckle escapes her lips.

"I know monsters …"

Tears streak her swollen face.

She strides forward, Sarah in hand. Sturdy. Unyielding.

Willow scrambles into Alder's arms. He holds her close. His pulse thrums vigorously.

Faith stands over the monster.

Her grip tightens around Sarah.

The glow swells.

She pauses—just for a moment.

Her breath catches. A tremor of grief, then there is only rage.

Faith clenches her jaw.

Her grip locks firm. Sarah's light blazes in response.

And then—

She swings again.

The war club slams into the beast's skull.

Light erupts with each strike.

Faith bludgeons the Windigo.

Again.

It reaches out, but looks like it's being held back.

She cracks the weapon against its head again, breaking off one of the monster's knife-like teeth.

Then again, against the side of the Windigo's head.

Again—

Thwack.

Whiff. Thwack. Whiff. Craaaaack.

Faith screams—a raw, otherworldly war cry that drowns out the Windigo's shrieks.

"YEAAAAA ..."

Again.

The Windigo goes limp.

Again.

"...AAAAAHHHHHHH."

Again.

Faith stops her beatdown. All goes silent.

She lingers over the Windigo, chest heaving, lip trembling. She sniffles once, and her voice thickens in her throat.

"Like the others ..."

She grips Sarah tighter, sneering. A ghostly aura rises along her arms, climbing across her chest, arcing around her. Faith's entire presence glows.

"... pathetic ... weakness hiding behind ... CRUELTY!"

She grits her teeth and swallows a trembling breath.

Behind her, Alder rises, holding Willow tight against his chest. Because of their bond, he feels renewed.

The Windigo's head twists toward him as it lies prone. Then, it speaks—the voice of his mother.

"Aldi ... I miss you."

Alder mutters, "Ma?"

184

The creature continues, "They say it's cancer ... No darkness, as long as I have my little light of mine ..."

Alder sets Willow down. She quickly grabs at his hand, clawing to stay close.

He's entranced.

"Mama ... ?" He snivels. "I'm here, Mama ... I'm s-sorry ... Ma ...?"

Alder steps toward the creature slowly, releasing Willow's hand.

The moment he does, the Windigo lunges, its razored hand and writhing appendages snatching toward Willow.

Alder's left leg buckles. He stumbles, but Faith's strong hand clamps his shoulder.

She yanks him back.

Without hesitation, Faith strides past him and slams her foot down on the Windigo's reaching arm.

It shrieks.

Faith lifts Sarah above her head—the pointed end aimed down at the monster's head. The Windigo tries to stand, but something holds it in place. An unseen force.

"Like the others ... you're a fucking joke."

Her voice is a verdict.

Light shimmers down the engraved green feather, glimmering like a magic-imbued emerald.

The hissing sound of static electricity builds. The light crackles and sparks, dancing around Faith.

Every hair on Alder's body stands on end.

Sarah hums in Faith's hands.

She tightens her hold. The war club arcs above her head. Green bolts shoot from both ends.

Faith rears back—

And drives the pointed end down.

Right between the monster's splintered spray of antlers.

The tip bursts from its gaping mouth, a blazing glow spilling between its knifed teeth.

Alder locks eyes with the creature. The fires flicker—then die.

The greed.

The hate.

No … the apathy.

All of it siphons into the war club.

The Windigo's slimy tendrils whip out—snap. They spasm in a grotesque, convulsing dance. Then they shrivel, peeling away in long, glistening strands.

They drop off, hissing the moment they hit the floor, quickly congealing into a thick, bubbling sludge that dries, hardens, and crumbles. It breaks down into fine black sands that blow about the floor. The grains of sand break down further.

Until there's nothing left.

Sarah's glow fades.

Faith staggers. Sarah slips from her grasp. Her breath catches—shallow, uneven. Her hand flutters to her side, fingers twitching like they're trying to keep something inside from breaking free.

A soft, pained moan slips from her lips—then she drops. No bracing. She falls beneath the dead weight of her own body.

Sarah clatters to the floor beside her. Its last ember of light sputters—then it goes dark.

Alder bellows, "FAITH!" He barely has time to react as his own pain erupts. He reaches for Faith just as his own body gives out.

A shade is drawn—pulled over as rainbow-stockinged legs at the end of the hallway twist in his vision.

Everything tumbles. The left leg gives out.

The last thing he hears is hurried squeaking—feet on slick linoleum.

"Dr. P?"

A small, scared whisper.

Darkness.

CHAPTER NINE

"Down here!" a muffled female voice calls.

Footsteps—punctuated by the sound of squeaking shoes—approach fast, then stop.

The voice is close now, right against Alder's ear, but it still sounds dull and distant.

"Doc, I called them. The critical care chopper is here. Don't move."

Alder blinks, his mind sluggish, his body heavy.

Then he registers who it is.

Russ.

She survived.

She must have been unconscious before, but she survived and she called in for help.

That girl can do anything!

Alder no longer feels pain. His headache is so severe, it's become something else entirely—emptiness.

Like he's trapped inside a mason jar, and the world outside is warped through prismatic, blinding light.

He doesn't feel his body being lifted from the cold linoleum.

He doesn't feel the shift in his weight.

He can barely hear. Barely see.

Even the rotting smell of the Windigo has faded away.

"W-w—" he tries to ask for Willow.

Russ's voice sounds far away. "She's OK, Doc. She's with me. We'll see you in Duluth!"

A man's voice asks, "Are you OK?"

Russ's reply sounds distant. "I'm good. Just got knocked the eff out."

She pauses, then replies softly, "Please—take care of them. C'mere, pun'kin."

"Will do … the other chopper's en route."

Warm blankets cocoon around Alder, tucked up to his neck—just tight enough to feel safe, but not claustrophobic.

Then he hears the high-pitched hum of the helicopter.

The ER doors blast open, and the bite of Minnesota cold nips at his exposed face as they wheel him outside.

Alder tries to sit up, but his strength is completely gone.

"F-f-f—" he gasps. "F-f-f—"

The deep voice of the critical care nurse muffles through the haze. "We got you, Dr. Peony. It's a quick flight to Duluth General. Thanks to Russ for giving a bang-up report on your condition! Get that one a raise!"

A loud bang, a jostle—he's lifted into the hold of the helicopter. The air inside is just as cold.

A grunt as the critical care nurse climbs in after him.

"Ready?" the nurse calls out. "Thank God that comet tail has cleared out. We wouldn't have been able to fly with that radio interference. Lucky!"

A voice above Alder's head replies, dull. "Yep—Bird Two is three minutes out. We need to clear the landing pad."

The nurse replies, "Roger that—let's take her up!"

The high-pitched hum builds, then deepens. Thicker. Thumping.

Alder feels it in his chest—heavy and rhythmic.

Thumph-thumph-thumph.

Alder hears music fade in, threading itself through the helicopter's thump—soft at first, then full-bodied.

"Ill Wind (You're Blowin' Me No Good)," as sung by Ella Fitzgerald. Not the same version as his favorite—Lee Morgan's—but it doesn't matter. This one feels right at the moment.

No one is playing it. The lullaby is a peace offering from his injured brain. The lyrics land gently.

Alder exhales. The breath stretches, endless.

Then—that familiar darkness blankets him yet again.

*   *   *

"Mother?" Alder feels.

Yes, Aldi.

"Is this the end?"

You only know of now.

To us, your then, your when, and your end—they are all woven into your now. There is no difference.

Yes, Aldi. This is an end—but not your own.

Every beginning is an end.

Every end … is a beginning.

Vibrant green breaks the empty darkness, revealing everything around him—which is everything. Every moment of his life, down to the microsecond. Each breath, each spilled glass of milk, each face slap, each innocent kiss. Every second of his life is splayed out like the leaves of a tree that stretches endlessly in all directions.

Something stands out. The moments he shared—every challenge, every shared triumph, every connection—are leaves growing close to the trunk. Their stems strongly attached—full of deep green life—drinking in the radiant rays of light.

But his failures, even his lonely victories, these leaves cling loosely to the ends of the branches, barely attached. Their stems yellow and withering. They refuse the soft nurturing beams of the light. Some leaves here have already fallen, lost to the dark abyss below.

The tree stands, rooted in the darkness—yet from every direction other than the abyss, photons of light wave and dance toward the receiving foliage, passing through it. Inside, molecules are activated, tilted, and rearranged; then released to join others and give life force to a all that breathe.

The leaves hum softly. A resonant frequency, tingling at the edge of the mind.

It feels like the molecules vibrate and swirl throughout our beings.

Certain frequencies can vibrate through our beings, an adjunct to healing. Bliss.

Like waking and finding your tiny sleeping body cradled by strong arms and carried through the hushed still of night.

Safety.

Alder finally accepts peace.

He feels freed from every burden, every grudge, every painful memory.

It's time.

He feels. "Please? Let me stay here?"

Only silence answers.

"Please! Are you there?" Alder reaches out, sensing.

Silence.

Sudden darkness swallows him. The silence also deepens. So much, it doesn't even ring in the ears.

That surge.

It rolls through Alder like a slow-moving current of electricity—followed by a garbled voice.

"OK—gimme a thumbs-up."

Light collects in his peripheral vision, as if he's wearing sun-rimmed spectacles.

Alder releases a deep, exhaled cough.

A man's voice. "Keep coughing. Get it on up—there you go!"

Alder's vision blurs in. His head feels heavy, throbbing, but the vision seems better.

He feels that surge of energy again, to his left and up his arm.

The energy feels weaker than before, almost negligible. The healing entanglement between them is waning, but that's OK, as his arm feels stronger on its own. He can feel the pressure of what he now sees is Willow Rose, clinging to him, her green eyes red and her face raw.

She mutters, "Dr. P."

Alder reaches his right hand over, pulling her tighter against him. She audibly sobs, pressing her face into his hospital gown.

Connection.

Hospital monitors beep in the distance from the hallway, but in here, there is just Willow Rose, and—

Russ.

She stands at the foot of the bed, clutching a paperback tight against her ribs and watching with an intent smile. "Hey, Doc."

Russ's head is wrapped in a pressure bandage. Beneath it, a faint swelling shadows her temple, bruises creeping past the edges like ink bleeding through fabric. Her left eye is nearly swollen shut.

To the right stand two men, the neurosurgeon and the respiratory therapist. They just pulled his breathing tube.

The neurosurgeon clears his throat.

"Dr. Peony. Dr. Faber."

"Hel—" Alder rasps, then coughs.

Dr. Faber waves his hand. "No worries, Alder. It's a pleasure. We've spoken on the phone before, but not in this context." He chortles. "So, yeah. I'm the one that fixed you up. You had a right-sided epidural hematoma, and we had to relieve the pressure.

"We performed a craniotomy. Your brain was close to herniating into your spinal canal. They got you here just in time. You've got a ways to go, but you may already notice some improvement in strength. You're young. I have every hope and expectation for significant improvement."

Alder groans and touches the right side of his scalp, which is under wads of wrapped gauze.

He understands: there was bleeding between his brain and skull. Enough pressure to shift his brain. They removed part of his skull to evacuate the blood and relieve that pressure.

Dr. Faber continues, "Yeah, there'll be a plate there. You may experience headaches, but for now—let's get you some of the good stuff—Dilaudid sound OK?"

A cough comes from the doorway, a soft female voice. "I think Doc needs some meds and rest, eh?"

Alder snaps his head to the doorway, disregarding the sloshing pain that accompanies that motion.

Faith.

There she is.

Alive.

She sits in a wheelchair with an orderly standing behind her.

Her left arm is wrapped in bandages, a rigid splint running its entire length. More dressings and splinting surround her legs, stark against the thin hospital gown.

Bruises and swelling shadow both eyes. Still, she is gorgeous.

The flutterbyes swarm inside Alder's chest.

He coughs.

"F-Faith ... you're—"

His voice breaks.

A wave of emotion chokes the words before they can form. Alder's eyes dampen.

Dr. Faber says, "Good idea. We'll keep that horde of reporters away as well. We are all grateful and indebted to you all for what you did—and we mourn your losses with you."

Russ walks over and scoops Willow's hand into hers. "C'mon, pun'kin. Let's go see if they got blueberry pancakes in the cafeteria. This place is big enough—I bet we can find some food fit for a hero."

Alder stops them. "Ru-Russ ..."

Russ turns. "Yeah, Doc?"

"How did you—" He hesitates. "How'd you know abou—"

She meets his eyes, replies before he can finish, "The war club?"

Alder nods.

Russ taps the Gayle Wynd paperback tucked under her arm, her thumb holding a place near the end. She grins. "You see these books I read? I saw that sonofabitch, and in my head, I heard boss music and choose your weapon." She shrugs. "I figured my best shot was to grab the glowy magic stick. The closer I got to you, the more it started shaking like crazy—could barely hold on to it."

Russ snickers and rubs her neck. "Oh, and I'm not some chickie-chick—it's gonna take more than a backhand to take me out! Heh." She gives Willow's hand a gentle tug. "Ready, pun'kin?"

Willow follows with no hesitation, her sidekick leading her out. On the way, she slows—just for a moment—to wrap her arms around Faith's neck in a quiet embrace.

Faith hums, soft and warm.

"Ooooh, thank you, my sweet baby."

Russ passes by Faith and drops her locket into her hand. Faith gets teary, her lips tensing.

She'd remembered to grab it from the hospital. She got what mattered out of there—them included.

As they all exit, the orderly wheels Faith to Alder's bedside.

"Can we have a moment?" she asks.

The orderly nods, stepping back toward the door. "Take your time."

He steps out, leaving the two alone.

Down the hall, an old man's voice shouts into a phone, his voice cracking with excitement.

"Hello? Yeah, I'm going home tomorrow! Hello? Pat … PAT!"

A muted *Quantum Leap* rerun flickers on the elevated TV. Through the slightly parted curtains, the last breath of twilight lingers, casting soft blue shadows across the floor.

Alder reaches for Faith's hand, his grip weak but steadier than before.

She stops him with a touch. "No—rest, love. We'll work on your strength later."

He exhales, letting the truth settle. Thinking about his planned return home.

There is no one back home.

There is no real home at all.

Only the place he was raised—then fled. Chicago.

A city that hums with the ghosts of old mistakes. Where trouble waits like an open door.

"Hey ..."

Faith's voice is soft, but it reaches through the fog.

She guards her side—careful, slow. A chest tube. The plastic glints under fluorescent lighting, taped in place to keeping her lung from collapsing—a reminder of what she's survived.

Alder turns, ignoring the sloshing pain behind his eyes. She is there. Big brown eyes, watching him, pulling him in.

"I don't expect—" His words slip, thin and tired.

Faith tilts her head. "Hey, I'm not going anywhere. Are you?"

Her sweet, honey voice. Her question settles deep.

Is she asking him to stay? Can this place—this wild, eerie, pine-spiked wilderness—be something more than a stop along the way?

The thought curls inside him.

He looks at Faith—this woman, this kind and quiet force.

He thinks of both her and Willow—of waking up to something real.

A tentative smile tugs at his lips. He exhales.

"Tssh."

The nurse steps into the room, a syringe in hand. His Dilaudid.

Alder exhales. The pain will dull soon.

Faith watches as the nurse preps the medication for an IV push, then leans in slightly, her soft voice whispering, "Sweet dreams, Aldi."

He smiles, his eyes growing heavy.

The world tilts as the drug drifts through his veins, warmth blooming in his body. He feels light. Euphoric. The pain dissolves, drifting away like a wisp in the wind.

Alder lets go.

Just before the darkness takes him, footsteps approach. A woman's voice appears.

"Faith? Ms. Linden?"

Faith's reply sounds distant. "Hi ... yes?"

"Beautiful. Like the tree," the woman says. "Teena Adebar. CPS. We spoke briefly on the phone about Willow?"

"Yes ... oh, yes," Faith whispers, then exhales a quiet laugh. "Mind giving me a ride?"

"Of course."

Faith whispers, "To the right and down the hall."

The faint squeak of the wheelchair fades. Then nothing.

Alder drifts off.

He dreams about Willow's smiling face. In fact, he wonders if he dreamed Willow into existence. If she is some lingering echo from a life he's already lived, or a life he's yet to reach. She is familiar in ways he can't explain, like a fragmented memory, like the space between waking and sleeping, where everything is true and unreal at the same time.

CHAPTER TEN

Fluorescent lights flicker overhead, competing with the overcast gray light filtering through clear mosaic windows. A distorted brown-and-green pattern sways from the trees outside.

Pepto-Bismol pink walls surround a paradoxically cold-feeling physical therapy room. Equipment, balls, and mats are scattered throughout.

Alder stares at a tired old motivational poster that reads: "Success is a Quest." He chuckles as footsteps squeak behind his wheelchair—his therapist, Rob.

"Alright! Here we go. Let's see you lift a house today."

Alder mutters, "Let's start with my body first?"

The wheelchair comes to a stop. Rob locks the wheels.

"Doc—week three. This is all you!"

Alder gives a sarcastic thumbs-up. He struggles to push himself up with his left arm, his thumb trembling from the strain.

He scoots his left leg under himself and gives it everything he's got. It trembles too, but he pushes through.

As he gets nearly upright, he starts to fall—but Rob grabs ahold of the canvas belt around Alder's waist—pulling him the rest of the way.

Alder exhales sharply through pursed lips. Droplets of sweat stick to his forehead.

"Pheeew. Wooo. Thank you, my good sir!"

Rob replies, "That was mostly you! You've come far—you'll be line-dancing in no time."

"Ha! You got jokes!"

"I'm here all week!" Rob smiles, then adds, "Not you though …
Heading home tomorrow, I hear?"

Alder looks down at his hands, his left gripping a cane, most of his
weight shifting to the right.

"Yep … that time!"

"Hey, I wish you the best! After all you've been through … You're an
inspiration, Doc!"

Alder blushes and shakes his head, quiet and humble. "I don't know
about all of that, but thanks, Rob. Thanks for everything!"

"Not a worry. So, what's for lunch?"

Rob walks alongside Alder as he takes intentional and careful steps
out of the PT room, assisted by a silver cane.

The metallic tick of the cane echoes down the hallway.

* * *

Duluth International Airport buzzes. A suitcase lands heavy on the
scale—a dark hand steadies it.

The airline clerk scans the ticket. He sings. "Chi—caaah—gooo
… home?"

Alder dangles his cane on the edge of the checkin counter as he rifles
for his wallet. "Yep. Sweet home, Chicago."

"Wonderful."

"Just visiting. We'll be back in next week."

Faith steps up to the counter. "Babe, did you pack her hoodie? And
… you know … that?"

Alder smirks. "Of course."

He unzips his carry-on, revealing a green hoodie, neatly rolled. He
taps their checked luggage. "And wouldn't forget her."

Faith sighs, giving a soft smile and a head tilt. "Well, you know she's
gonna want that sweatshirt."

A tiny hand tugs at Alder's side.

Willow's smiling face appears, tilted up at the clerk. He winks at her, then returns his gaze to the monitor.

The clerk beams. "Oh! It's someone's birthday—four-eleven."

He grins wider. "Happy birthday, Mr. Peony!"

Willow giggles. "Dr. Peony." She twinkles. "It's my birthday too."

The clerk tilts his head, a contrived look of surprise spreading across his face.

"Oh, reeeeeally now? Look at that!"

He taps the keyboard in rhythm as he says with staccato, "What … a … coin … ci … dence. Synchronicity, even!"

Alder and Faith share a flickering glance at each other, then snicker it off.

The clerk tears off the ticket. "Well, you three enjoy the Windy City, and we shall see you on … your return."

"Thanks!" Alder dips his head and raises an eyebrow.

He finishes signing his slip—still clumsy with his left hand, but he's getting there.

Still easier than those weeks writing with that rasshole right hand.

He double-takes as he grabs his cane and slings his carry-on bag over one shoulder. He taps the cane down but barely leans into it.

"I can't wait till you two see the old house. I can finally do right by it—thanks to Mama Curlie. Who knew she was loaded?" He chuckles.

"No wonder she never took my money—she wanted to leave it all to us."

Alder glances toward Faith and Willow. "And my mother … she'd be down with this. Rest her soul."

Faith takes his right hand, interlocking her fingers with his. Then she does the same with his left, her soft brown eyes hovering before him.

Her cheek dimple says hello.

They share a quiet kiss.

Faith's eyes flutter closed.

She whispers, "She was proud of you … the whole time, through it all. So are we."

She opens her eyes, smiling gently.

Alder flushes.

He exhales, smiling softly with a subtle head shake.

Willow darts beneath Faith's arm, and the three of them drift through the airport terminal.

The aroma of cinnamon rolls, coffee, and buttery popcorn fills the air.

Overhead TVs flicker as news tickers roll along the bottoms of the screens. Alder's eyes scan the headlines—most of them about Comet Goodwin—and surrounding events.

Nessie Slayers! Scottish Family Saves Town from Cryptid!

Nearby magazines and tabloids shout in bold type:

• Luna Goodwin and her comet-themed dog wear!

• Parallel Universes: Fact or Fiction?

• Echo Entanglement and You? Tests Underway.

Alder peeks over at Willow—high-stepping, bouncing, hand in Faith's.

AB+ and untypeable. A perfect match.

She's lost enough—an entire life.

He will protect what she's gained … and what she gave to him: a new life.

The three pass a young man on a laptop. He adjusts his baseball cap, then twists the cap off a Coke bottle as his head cranes toward the overhead screen.

He fumbles. The cap tumbles to the floor.

As he bends to catch it, his earbud cord yanks from his laptop.

Music spills into the air.

"Shark Attack" by The Wailing Souls.

That damned song.

A slow, crawling chill threads through Alder's ribs.

The floor hums—vibrates.

His eyes flick to the conveyor belt behind the counter, where their checked bags slip into the dark baggage abyss.

A glow blooms within—first faint, then swelling—until it lights the space beyond.

On the other side of the belt, a group of men stand frozen, their faces bathed in green light, watching with confused wonder. Sarah.

The overhanging TVs flicker. A faint pixelated image of a waxing partial solar eclipse stutters on the screen, fragmented by digital noise. At the bottom, the distorted caption scrolls in broken text:

Spec—Report ... Partial Solar Eclip—by Rogue—anet? Orphan moo—? President George W.—ush overheard: Not this s—again!

On another screen, pixelated footage of a tsunami spilling across a coastal city.

A familiar shock ripples up Alder's arm—a surge of warmth, an internal tsunami crashing against the walls of his soul.

The weakness in his leg, gone.

Then he realizes he's not the only one feeling it.

Faith and Willow both jolt upright. They all look at each other.

Willow's voice tightens. "Dr. P?"

Alder grips his cane, tosses it up, and catches it effortlessly in his left hand. Easy.

Something stirs beneath his skin—warm, electric. His senses sharpen. His tension dissolves.

The photon-warm current flows between him, Faith, and Willow, their hands clasped tight.

It's back.

Faith's eyes flick to him. Then Willow.

The healing energy of entanglement had left them ...

But now ...

It's back.

They felt it, you felt it too.

This is our world.

She was gifted to us, and us to her.

So, let's protect her.

Peace is not stillness.

Together, yeah?

At every end ... there is a beginning.

AFTERWORD

Thank you for spending time with me. I hope you've enjoyed the story. It started out as a wacky thought after a tiny knock at my cabin door while in the woods of Wild Rose, WI.

I like to think that stories arriving this way aren't just products of my thoughts, but transcribed whispers, not heard by proper ears, but coming from another place. I feel humbly thankful for the opportunity to hear them. And I hope the whispers never end—I'd love to do this for years to come.

While writing *Willow Rose*, I found a peace, but my heart wasn't still— it swayed between heaviness and hope. My own victories and pains, as is often the case when writing, became intertwined with the characters.

I trudged through all this mumbo-jumbo to share a belief that we are all entangled. Every being shares a deep connection, deeper than any root can burrow, and extending far beyond the reaches of the most distant visible celestial body.

Many of our pains—and feelings of hopelessness—emerge when we forget our connections, or try to replace *We* with the illusion of *Me*.

Nothing thrives alone in this universe, which itself exists as a We. A collection of matter and mystery, all twisting and swirling about. It's OK if things crash into each other once in a while—that happens when you're not alone.

Atoms coalesce to form molecules. Molecules join in lattice handshakes to become cells. Those cells work together to form organs. Then the organs join to animate this splendid thing called life.

But we're often blind to that wonder. We place so much stock in what we can see—and in doing so, overlook the beauty of what truly holds it all together.

Every flourishing thing is part of something larger. Our beautiful planet came together to form a perfect, self-sustaining home for all that swim, fly, and creep about.

This world tirelessly flashes with a brilliant and limitless hope—found in every flapping wing, smiling face, and tight, lingering hug. The light of hope exists in every tool of caring, no matter how small. Even within the fell wood that led Mr. Benoit and became Sarah.

Empathy isn't a weakness. In this world, it's resistance.

If we are just willing to take hold of another hand, we can face anything that sneaks out of the void.

With heart,

M. Kevin Hayden

stay together

www.ingramcontent.com/pod-product-compliance
Lightning Source LLC
Chambersburg PA
CBHW050327110726
47899CB00007B/2407